W9-BGY-664

J.2
7pts

waiting for christopher

waiting for christopher

.
.
.

a novel by

Louise Hawes

CANDLEWICK PRESS
CAMBRIDGE, MASSACHUSETTS

First edition 2002

Library of Congress Cataloging-in-Publication Data

Hawes, Louise.
Waiting for Christopher : a novel / by Louise Hawes.
p.   cm.
Summary: Shortly after moving with her mother to Florida, a lonely, fourteen-year-old bibliophile is reminded of her infant brother who died and decides to care for an abused, abandoned child with help from a new friend.
ISBN 0-7636-1371-1
[1. Parenting — Fiction. 2. Mother and child — Fiction. 3. Child abuse — Fiction. 4. Abandoned children — Fiction. 5. Friendship — Fiction. 6. Books and reading — Fiction.] I. Title.
PZ7.H3126 Wai 2002
[Fic] — dc21   2001043476

2   4   6   8   10   9   7   5   3   1

Printed in the United States of America

This book was typeset in MBembo.

Candlewick Press
2067 Massachusetts Avenue
Cambridge, Massachusetts 02140

visit us at www.candlewick.com

For Lily, born in love

*You will not come? You will not be my comforter, my
rescuer? My deep love, my wild woe, my frantic prayer,
are all nothing to you?*

—Charlotte Brontë, JANE EYRE

*She didn't read books so she didn't know that she was the
world and the heavens boiled down to a drop.*

—Zora Neale Hurston, THEIR EYES WERE WATCHING GOD

.
.
•

prologue

Whenever she could, Feena brought Christopher
something from outside. She sneaked in when he was
supposed to be napping, when the steady thump
thump thump *of the washer meant their mother was*
in the basement, folding warm sheets, baby clothes
and diapers, T-shirts that said things like I ♥ MY
CAT *or* U.S. BREATHING TEAM. *Feena knew what*
the shirts said, because she'd asked over and over
until she'd learned them all by heart. Which made
her mother smile and her father laugh and pick her
up. "Forget kindergarten," he'd tell her. "You're
going straight to college."

Sometimes she brought her brother little things, like a moth wing or an elderly dandelion, all whiskers and silk. They were pieces of the world she knew he needed to look at and touch, things her mother didn't allow in the nursery. She slipped them between the bars of his crib, then pushed them to where he could see.

Bigger presents, like the rusty sand pail she'd found, with a yellow handle and a circus seal painted on the side, she would drag with her to the top of the crib rail, then throw herself over, landing beside the baby, both of them laughing loudly until she put a hand over his mouth. "We'll get time-outs," she'd warn him, suddenly stern. "If you don't be quiet, I won't get you any more stuff."

But as soon as she uncovered his mouth, Christopher would start giggling and wiggling again, like a wind-up toy you couldn't stop. Feena figured he smiled at her so much because she was the only one who guessed how awful it was not to be able to walk around by yourself. Because she brought him bits of life that hadn't had the fun washed out of them.

She knew she was four years older than Christy, so she decided she would have to wait that long for him to catch up. But that was okay. It was worth it. Because when he got to be as old as she was, Feena wouldn't need to be a big sister anymore. She'd never *have to* Wait just a minute *or* Keep those dirty hands to yourself *or* Let the baby sleep, for god's sake, can't you see I'm tired.

As soon as her brother could walk, she'd show him the dead bird behind the garage, a wet, ragged hole where one of its eyes should be, its feet curled so tight you couldn't open them, no matter what. When he learned to talk, she'd tell him about the sneakers with red laces in the store that had elevators. Feena knew he'd be mad at Mommy. "She was bad," he'd say, "not to let you buy those beautiful sneaks. Your feet grow fast; they'll be big enough soon."

The day she found the pinecones, she waited a long time, hoping her mother would come out of Christy's room and go downstairs. She stood just outside his door, opening and closing her hands over them. She guessed he would like the way they smelled, but she worried they might leave sticky patches of brown sap on his cheeks, like the ones inside her palms.

Why was her mother taking so long? Wasn't there any laundry to do? She squeezed her fingers over the sharp, shaggy points of the cones and watched tiny half-moons appear and disappear in her skin. Was Christy going to skip his nap today? She tried to see through the hair-thin crack between the door and its frame, but it was dark in there, as if she'd closed her eyes and was looking through her lids. When she heard someone crying, she knocked on the door, but nothing happened. The sobs grew heavy and hard, not at all like her brother's high, stuttery wail. That was when she'd jammed all three pinecones into one hand and pushed open the door.

Some surprises are good, like a ponytailed doll for your birthday. And some surprises, like the time Daddy spanked her and left the red mark of his hand on her leg, make you feel as if you've just swallowed too much ice, as if you're going to stay cold forever. Now, standing just inside the door, Feena saw so many people in Christopher's room, she couldn't tell which of them was crying. How had they gotten there? Had they all tiptoed upstairs while she was watching cartoons?

At first, she thought it might be her mother who was crying. She tried to see past the forest of trouser legs and jeans and shimmering nylons to the baby's crib. He would be scared, she knew, with so many visitors at once. She pushed her way through a few of the clustered adults but was stopped before she could reach her brother. A woman with very red lips and a scratchy jacket picked her up. Feena arched back over the woman's shoulder, stretching toward the crib. "Christopher?" she called, dropping two of the pinecones. "Where's Christy?"

"Your brother's not here, dear," the woman told her, holding Feena's legs too tight, carrying her

4

toward the door. "Aunty Bell's going to take you outside for a bit. Would you like that?"

From her uncomfortable perch, Feena considered the woman's face, its porous, vaguely familiar contours. Then she stared down at the single pinecone left in her hand. It was probably too prickly, anyway, she decided. She would bring him a tuft of the shiny green needles instead. "Where's Christy?" she asked again.

"He's gone to heaven," the woman said, mashing Feena against the hairy jacket. "He's gone to heaven to play with the angels."

But Christopher wasn't playing with angels. Her mother explained things to Feena later, after the crying had stopped and everyone who didn't live with them had gone back to their own houses. She told Feena that sometimes babies stop breathing and no one knows why. Even though it's usually old people who die, she said, every once in a while, a baby dies, too. When Feena remembered the bird she'd found and asked if Christopher still had both his eyes, her mother made a strange, thin bleating sound. Feena had never heard anything like it before, and she tried to make it herself, rocking back and forth in the dim light from the hall, before her father came to put her to bed.

Usually they read a book, but that night Daddy didn't open the one they were already halfway through. Instead, he sat beside her in the dark and told a story, a story about how Christopher was going to sleep under the ground. About how the three of them could go and talk to him, even though they wouldn't be able to see him or pick him up or play so-o-o-o-o big.

And that's what they did—every Friday, as soon as her father got home from work. She knew when it was Christy's day, because Daddy didn't walk into the kitchen and open the refrigerator and drink right out of the orange-juice carton. He didn't yell, "Feena, Feena, where you beena?" and pull her onto his lap. Instead, he stayed in the car and honked the horn until Feena and her mother had grabbed their sweaters and gotten in beside him.

Each time they drove to the cemetery, she brought along something for her brother to play with. When she remembered about the pine needles, her father helped her scatter them around the stone with Christopher's name cut into it. "How will he get them?" Feena worried. "How will he know they're here?"

Her father's forehead was so pale, she could see a spider web of blue veins under his skin. "He'll know," he told her. He patted the ground once, then stood up. "He has to, Feenie. He just has to."

But Feena wasn't so sure. The only thing she knew for certain was that her brother was to be pitied *now more than ever. Being in a little cage with arms and legs that hadn't learned to work yet was bad. Lying still behind the garage, with only one eye and feet as blue as nails, that was horrible, too. But sleeping under the ground, cold and alone and afraid of the dark—that was the worst thing she could imagine.*

"No," she said, when her father tried to pull her to her feet. She folded her arms, turned away from him.

"No," she insisted when her mother doubled back from the car and stooped beside her, patting her shoulder, smoothing her hair. "I'm not going." Pine needles pricked her legs, and tears, warm as baby's milk, worked their way to the corners of her mouth. "I'm waiting for Christopher," she said. "I'm waiting right here till he wakes up."

one

.

.

.

Moving from Connecticut to Florida had sounded like a good idea last year. But last year, moving to Katmandu would have had its appeal. After skipping eighth grade and going straight to high school, after being catapulted from the few friends she'd made at Byrd Middle School into the relentless fashion-and-personality meat grinder of Edgemoor Senior High, Feena would have gone to the ends of the earth to escape another semester of humiliation and loneliness.

That, of course, was before she'd seen the house her mother had rented for them. "It's a little out of the way," Lenore Harvey had explained, slipping coffee mugs into blister packs, nesting them in one of the cardboard cartons they'd talked the A&P manager out of flattening. "But it's got two bedrooms and it's affordable and"—a rare half smile—"we'll never be cold again!"

None of this had been a lie, Feena conceded now, studying the sliver of grass and the tiny box-shaped house with its arched door like the brick oven in a pizzeria.

Her mother had never liked city life, but after the terrorist attack in New York, she'd decided they needed to live thousands of miles from skyscrapers and traffic.

She had laughed when she'd christened their new home "the Pizza Hut," but it was hard to look at it without wishing she were anywhere else, even back in Connecticut.

Inside, the house was mean and cramped, with three small rooms that were nearly identical: same shape, same color, same postage-stamp window half filled with an air conditioner that proved next to useless against Florida's roiling, steamy heat.

And the outside was worse. Much worse. From the moment she'd seen it, Feena knew the Pizza Hut would seal her fate, confirm her role as social outcast. No matter how sophisticated or funny or charming she made herself, no matter how much mousse she used or how well she fitted in at her new school, she was bound to be a Loser with a capital *L* as soon as anyone found out where she lived.

The tiny house was squeezed between a large asphalt parking lot—where Feena now sat in their '89 Chevy, running the air and reading her favorite novel for the umpteenth time—and Ryder's Fun Land, where six giant flying teacups were just slowing down, the one with the red handle, like always, finishing on top. In front of the house was a narrow strip of earth in which, before she knew better, Feena had tried to grow a garden, had spent weeks propping up seedlings, watering, weeding.

...Amidst the drenched piles of rubbish, spring had cherished vegetation: grass and weed grew here and there between the stones and fallen rafters. And oh! where meantime was the hapless owner of this wreck? In what land?

As Jane Eyre pondered the blackened remains of Thornfield Hall, Feena had only to raise her eyes a few inches to find a far less romantic ruin. It was an overstatement to call Ryder's an amusement park. A ten-hole miniature golf course and three kiddie rides on a backwater highway were certainly a joke, but nobody Feena knew was laughing: not Feena, when stragglers trooped across the yard, crushing the watercress shoots and baby lettuce as soon as they showed aboveground; not old Peter Milakowski, who'd bought the park when Route 56 was the only shore road out of Ocala, and who'd watched the new four-lane thruway make him a failure overnight; not even the handful of sticky, whiny toddlers whose mothers scooped them out of shopping carts and car seats and highchairs, only to plop them into fiberglass tugboats and fire engines and teacups.

As for the golf course, Feena had never seen anyone besides Mr. Milakowski set foot on it. Every morning, he swept the strip of green carpeting with an old broom, then put out three rows of golf clubs, their silver shafts glinting from under the roof of the small ticket booth. Carefully, he arranged pencils and scorecards, enough for a dozen players.

Who never came. Each night, Mr. Milakowski turned off the machine that moved a plastic tiger's tail back and forth, back and forth across the narrow opening to the tenth hole, pulled all the clubs inside the booth, and locked the door. "Golf," he told Feena whenever she helped, matching the careful pace of his arthritic fingers, slipping the clubs one by one into the storage stand. "Where is a kid who really likes golf?" He stretched the word out so that it sounded more like "guuullf."

"Only if I can pay for fancy volcanoes that are shooting steam. Only if I buy talking robots and pirate ships does anyone care about this game."

But in his countenance I saw a change: that looked desperate and brooding—that reminded me of some wronged and fettered wild beast or bird, dangerous to

approach in his sullen woe. The caged eagle, whose
gold-ringed eyes cruelty has extinguished, might look
as looked that sightless Samson.

Her mother would be furious if she were to come
home early from work and find Feena running the
engine like this. But it was such a relief to feel the frigid
rush from the vents, to read as the air conditioner
hummed, to let Rochester's tragic figure overwhelm the
comedy of living where she lived, being who she was.

And who was she, anyway? A fourteen-year-old
misfit with too much red hair and skin so pale it looked
as though she spent her days under a rock (which, if she
wanted to avoid being blistered by the Florida sun,
wouldn't have been a bad idea). While other girls were
confident and quick, with knowing, fluid bodies and an
endless supply of MTV patter, Feena felt trapped by her
chalky flesh, her cautious, unreliable brain that arrived
at the perfect retort, the ideal comeback after it was too
late and nobody else cared.

"How come you're always alone, Feen?" Feena
knew exactly what her mother would say if she were to
find her here. "Aren't kids your age supposed to run in
packs? You never do anything but turn pages."

Was that any worse, Feena wondered, than watching television every waking second?

Ever since she'd seen two of the tallest buildings in
the world sliced like bread by airplanes, Feena hadn't

been able to watch TV at all. But her mother had gone to the other extreme, burying her head in the soaps.

How many times had Feena lost out to *Days of Our Lives* and *As the World Turns*? How many confessions had she made, how many jokes had she told, to the back of her mother's head? "Can't you see I'm tired?" Lenore would say, tiny, microscopic versions of the characters on the big-screen Sony moving inside the lenses of her glasses. "Honest, Feen. Weekends are the only time I've got to relax. Can't you just leave me be?"

Rochester and Jane. Tess of the d'Urbervilles and Angel. Heathcliff and Cathy in *Wuthering Heights*. Maxim de Winter, haunted by the mysterious Rebecca. Maybe, Feena admitted, the characters she adored were just as storm tossed, every bit as overblown as the soap opera stars her mother followed. But at least they were partly Feena's creations, their faces and bodies and voices filled out by her imagination. She could take them with her, read them into life in an idling car or a boring class. There was no limit to when or where or how much she could love them.

Love wasn't too strong a word for it, either. Whether Edward Rochester was real or not seemed irrelevant in the face of how much he meant to her. While everything around her—her brother, her father, her home—faded away, Rochester remained, fixed and bright. She couldn't remember Christopher's face anymore, could hardly reconstruct her father's. But Brontë's hero was easy to see, to call up whenever she needed him.

He was much older than she was, of course, but not as old as Mr. Milakowski. Probably her father's age. Broad-chested, craggy, tortured. Even though the one photo her dad had sent in the eight years since he'd left showed a slender-bordering-on-skinny man with a sloppy smile that didn't remotely suggest tragedy, Feena always pictured Rochester with her father's storm-green eyes and uncombable copper-colored hair.

And if Tyler Harvey—tall and funny, with a laugh like deep water—could look at Feena the way he used to when she was little, could hold her to him, then push her away and lock on to her eyes as if what he saw was the most wonderful thing in the world and he never wanted to stop looking, why then, that explained how Rochester could fall in love with his plain Jane.

The muscular hand broke from my custody; my arm was seized, my shoulder—neck—waist—I was entwined and gathered to him.

"Is it Jane? What is it? This is her shape—this is her size—"

"And this her voice," I added. "She is all here: her heart, too. God bless you, sir! I am glad to be so near you again."

"Jane Eyre!—Jane Eyre," was all he said.

How strange to sit here, Feena thought, to glance up from the page where anguish and loss had resolved themselves into a moment like a sigh—the moment when Rochester, blind and helpless as a wounded lion, stood once more beside his little Jane—to peer now through the dust-specked window of the Chevy at three mothers who held out their arms and lifted three cranky little girls from their perches on the whirling teacups.

Not three girls, actually, Feena realized. Distracted, she closed the book and studied the child climbing out of the red-handled cup. He was a boy, she saw now, with tumbled blond hair that would have done justice to a baby Cinderella or Sleeping Beauty. He seemed to be two, maybe three, not old enough yet to be embarrassed by the luxuriant curls his mother had left uncut.

Feena couldn't hear anything beyond the air conditioner's breezy whine, but she wondered idly if the child was laughing or crying. His expression was ambiguous—either torture or delight. Either exhilaration from the speedy blur of the ride, or fear at having been stranded, spun into orbit all alone.

As she led him away, the little boy's mother talked, her mouth shaping large, exaggerated urgencies. Feena had no idea what she was saying. The woman's expression was as hard to interpret as her son's. She might have been angry, or just sad and serious. Sometimes Feena's own mother got that very same look on her face when she was worried, trying to discuss something important with Feena. Other times, though, the look was a prelude, a cue that Lenore was working her way into a stiff drink or a good cry. Or a long, furious tirade—at her boss in the department of motor vehicles or at Feena, whom she accused of failing utterly to appreciate all the sacrifices and hard work Lenore had suffered on her account.

But now as Feena watched the two other children and their mothers head toward the parking lot, the ambiguity was resolved. The woman hit her little boy. Then hit him again.

Feena sat hypnotized as the woman raised her arm, lowered it, raised it. At a distance, from behind the car window, she had a certain grace. As if she were dancing or beating a drum. Keeping time, she struck the boy over and over.

The child's response was to stiffen. Like Feena, he remained frozen, but unlike her, he turned away. He assumed the stance of a fighter in a clinch, his arms protecting his face, his knees slightly bent as if ready for flight. The flurry of blows couldn't be as hard as they looked, Feena decided, or he would have fallen by now.

Coming out of her trance, she turned off the car's engine and opened the door. At first, the only sound she heard was the tinny jumble of recorded music that came from each of the rides. The ten tugboats—yes, she had counted them; what else did she have to do all summer?—sailed around a ring of shallow greasy water to a tune that sounded like "Anchors Aweigh." The teacups spun to a Muzak version of "It's a Small World," and the fire trucks' endless circling was punctuated, not with actual music, but with a series of short, deep siren blasts like a stuck car horn.

When she'd reached the edge of the lot, though, Feena picked out another sound, a high-pitched angry voice. She was close enough now to see that the mother was young, with a pretty, round face that didn't match her voice at all, and that the little boy was unusually dirty.

"One more time, mister," the sweet-faced woman yelled. She had stopped slapping, had folded her arms. "You cry one more time, and I'm leaving you right here." She was heavy, her jeans shiny along the seams, her arms solid, startling in their pinkness.

Either because he couldn't stop or because he didn't believe her, the child kept howling. His misery was unmistakable now, a wail of despair that rose above the canned sirens. His face was hidden by the flopping sleeves of his tee, by his muddy elbows and arms. Only the bright curls showed above his fighter's crouch.

"What did I tell you, Christopher?" the woman screamed, raising her volume to match his. "What did I just tell you?" She glared at the child, daring him to continue crying. When he did, she turned, shrugged into her purse strap, and strode off without looking back.

Maybe it was the name his mother had called him, or maybe it was the sight of the boy's small, sober face as he lowered his arms to watch her walk away. Feena didn't stop to ask herself why. In an instant, she was moving toward him, streaking past the Pizza Hut, trampling the last of the watercress, and then scrambling up the chainlink fence between them.

two

.

.

.

She had just scaled the fence, its links circling her fingers like so many rings, when the boy's mother came back. Feena, her world chopped into tiny, mesh octagons, watched the woman hold out one hand, watched the child take it.

It was such a simple, clean negotiation. Both mother and son seemed to know their parts, seemed to have played them over and over. Feena felt relieved, as if she'd been watching some sort of ritual, a performance that had now come to an end. She dropped from the fence and turned toward the gate.

Perhaps, she decided, she'd go help Mr. Milakowski. It was nearly closing time. The canned music continued to blare from the loudspeakers, but the fire engines and teacups sat stalled and empty. Passengerless, the boats still fitfully circled their narrow course as if, Feena thought, kids had jumped ship in the middle of their rides.

She was nearly at the gate when she heard it again. Sharp, outraged yelling. She saw them off to her right, the mother bending over the boy. "Didn't I tell you?" the woman asked, punctuating her question with a slap at the circle of arms that once again protected the little boy's face. "Didn't I say, you keep blubbering, I'm out of here?"

But the child kept crying, howling louder and louder until the woman slapped him again. "You don't believe me, huh? You think all I got to do is stand around while you put on a show?"

More howls. More slaps. "It'll get dark. Everyone'll go home and you'll be here all by yourself." A significant pause, lingering, slapless, to let this picture sink in. "Just keep right on bawling, Mister Smarty, and see what happens."

Under his raised arms, the child didn't try to stop but yielded completely to the sobs that shook him like tremors. "That's it, Christopher. I've taken all the noise from you I'm gonna take." The woman straightened, turned sharply as a cadet. She strode through the gate, and as she brushed past Feena, their eyes met for a split second. But the woman looked away and marched determinedly toward the parking lot.

Feena waited just inside the gate now, watching the boy named Christopher, wondering if she should approach him. He stood unmoving, rooted to the spot as if he'd been there forever. Staring past Feena at his vanishing mother, his expression wasn't fearful so much as patient, waiting for the dark she'd promised him.

Just when Feena had decided to try to talk to him, to pick him up and carry him to Mr. Milakowski, his mother, yelling as she came, moved in on them again. Apparently, she'd never intended to leave at all, was interested only in tormenting the toddler. Now you see me, now you don't. Feena was furious, even if the little boy wasn't.

This time, the woman didn't even glance at Feena, seemed not to notice anyone but her son. "Look at that." There was a nasty, teasing edge to her voice. "Mister Smarty-pants is Mister Scaredy-pants now." Hands on hips, she loomed over him, looking down. "Guess now you know what happens to bad boys, don't you?

"Guess you're going to let Mommy be, right?" In the space she left him between taunts, the boy held both his arms out to her. Wordless, fighting tears, he begged her to pick him up. But she batted his hands away.

"What happens to bad boys who keep bothering

Mommy?" For a second, in an instinctive reflex, he held his arms up again, then quickly pulled them back, stood with them at his sides, only his face raised to her.

"Come on." She sighed theatrically, adjusted her purse strap again. Then she grabbed one of his hands and dragged him toward the gate. "I got stuff to do."

"Kids," Peter Milakowski said, closing the brightly painted door of the miniature-golf booth, fishing a padlock from his jacket pocket. "You have it easy. You don't know." He waved the tiny lock at Feena, who, with nothing to do now that the clubs were secured for the night, stood with her hands in her jeans pockets, letting the old man talk. "When I was a kid, what did I know?

"Nothing, same as you," he answered himself. He smiled sadly, the thin skin under his eyes working itself into intricate crepe-paper ridges. "You think your corn flakes, they come from nowhere? Your clothes, you think they don't cost money?"

"Mr. Milakowski." Feena looked for an opening, a way past his philosophizing, the bony reef of words that always surrounded him. "What if a kid has serious trouble with a parent? Like hitting and things."

"Hitting?" he asked. He shook his head. "What's hitting? Nothing, that's what. Your mother works hard, she gets tired, is all."

"But it's not me, really. It's—"

"You be thankful for only hitting. You be thankful you got a mother. Period."

She wanted to explain about Christopher. About the woman's fleshy arms, her baby's patient, empty eyes. But it was no use. The old man had an almost romantic notion of childhood, a conviction that real suffering belonged only to adults.

And maybe he was right, Feena told herself. Maybe it was no big deal. The boy wasn't starving, after all. His mother hadn't actually left him. There were other children all over the world, thousands and thousands of them, who were probably much worse off. Who had real problems, problems even Mr. Milakowski would have acknowledged.

Maybe, Feena decided as she headed back to the car, she was just bored. Looking for someone besides herself to feel sorry for. Someone with her dead brother's name. What sort of tragic novel did she think she was living, anyway?

She reached across the steering wheel, already burning hot, to retrieve her copy of *Jane Eyre*. It was a good thing that summer vacation was over, that school would start next week. By that time, she certainly wouldn't be bored anymore. She'd be too busy trying to be mellow and kick-ass all at once. Trying to hide her brains and her sloppy, wild heart.

Instinctively, Feena kept the book behind her as she pushed open the Pizza Hut's unlocked front door. Her mother, who must have caught an early bus, lay sprawled, shoeless, drink in hand, across the length of the couch. She didn't turn around when Feena came in, but remained facing the Sony. A thin, languorous arm with a gold watch at the wrist waved from the couch.

"Hey, Mom."

"Don't slam the door, Feen." Lenore's head turned a few degrees, one of her silver fish earrings glinting at Feena. On the screen, a man leaned over a woman in a hospital bed. "Darling," he said, "I can't bear to see you in pain."

Feena knew the drill, knew there was no point trying to interrupt the shows her mother taped for herself every day. "Some people gamble," she always told Feena. "Some people do drugs. Me? I need the soaps. Sue me."

As she passed the kitchen, Feena hoped her stomach would forget she'd had only a hard-boiled egg and celery for lunch. In her room, she reassured herself by looking at the new pink shirt she'd hung over her mirror. *New school,* she told herself. *New start.* She lifted the hanger, as if she might find something new in the glass underneath, too. But she didn't. In the second before she let the shirt fall back into place, she saw what she always did: the same thick horsy body, the same pasty moon face veiled with freckles. One egg and three celery stalks, she reminded herself crossly, couldn't be expected to make her hipless and hollow-cheeked overnight. She slipped the book into the bookcase by her bed, then stood in the doorway, looking over her mother's shoulder at the TV.

"What did you say?" A blond woman was talking to the same man who'd been in the hospital a moment before.

"I said," the man told her, "I don't care if Sarah never gets well. As long as it means you and I can be together."

The woman slapped him then, and the actor reeled backward, shocked and sheepish.

Feena wondered how they did it—made that dull, solid thud when she hit him. It sounded real. It sounded hard enough to hurt. "You're talking about my sister," the blond yelled. "I don't ever want to hear you say anything like that again."

Fade to commercial. "Mom?" Feena took a tentative step into the living room.

Lenore turned, resurfacing. She'd eaten or drunk most of her Sandy Mauve lip-gloss away, looked softer, prettier than when she'd left for work. She took a quick sip from the glass in her hand. "Lord, I wish I could edit out this junk. What's up, anyway?" She glanced at Feena now, eyebrows floating a little too high, mouth tight. Feena knew that look. *Make it quick,* the look said. *You've got until the bleach gets the stains out.*

"I saw this kid on the rides today."

"So?"

"So I was watching him and his mom. I thought she was—"

"Have you been shutting yourself up in the car again? For crying out loud, Feen, can't you find some friends instead of using up my gas?"

"Mom, what do you want me to do—go out to the highway and flag down cars? This place is not exactly crawling with potential playmates, you know." She glanced toward the window and Ryder's. "Unless you count preschoolers."

"What happens if I need to go shopping tomorrow?" Both of Lenore's fish were trembling, indignant. "What happens if the car won't start?"

"Don't cry," a new man told the blond woman on TV. He had gray hair and a soft, startled voice. "Please, don't cry."

Lenore pivoted, faced the screen. Both fish disappeared.

"Mom, I just—"

"Not now." Lenore waved the back of her hand at Feena.

"But I—"

"Shhhhh. Later." Another wave, smaller this time, as if she were swatting a fly off her shoulder.

three

•

•

•

Washanee Springs Regional was more and less than Feena had expected. More students, less attitude. The day after Labor Day, she found herself gliding invisibly as a ghost along the noisy low-ceilinged hallways. One student asked her where the bookstore was, and another apologized when he bumped her with his backpack, but most hardly noticed her at all. Relieved, she stopped worrying about what she was wearing, about the single pimple, blazing like a red star in the middle of her forehead.

Last year at Edgemoor, things had been different. She'd been the youngest person in school, and school had been a lot smaller. So small that she and Denise Northrup, the dark-haired, soft-spoken girl who'd been her friend from the first day, who loved books and lived outside of town in a log cabin, were typed from the start. They were in an accelerated English class, so they were "smart." They didn't have the right label patch on their jeans, so they were "nerds." Which meant that they sat with the other smart nerds in class, they ate at the smart nerd table in the cafeteria, and they walked home with the smart nerds after school. "It's a caste system," Denise told her. "And we're one step below the sacred cows."

But it wasn't like that here, where four separate districts fed into the same city-size high school. Feena felt a glorious, free-floating anonymity, lost among new jeans, old jeans, torn jeans. There were whites and blacks and Hispanics; preppies with collared shirts and razor-sharp parts in their hair; slow-eyed stoners, dressed in black; skinny kids with arms and legs that had outgrown the rest of them; heavy kids who shuffled down the halls without looking up; freaks and honeys, jocks and brains; and a few fine fools who didn't fit anywhere, who made their own rules.

Like Raylene Watson. Feena noticed her from the first day, envied the way the girl's calm fortified and protected her, the way she moved like an African goddess through the changing, mottled crew in the cafeteria. Without trying or caring, she was a force to be reckoned with. She spoke sparingly in class, but with a tongue of fire in the halls. She stood outside the school doors before opening bell with her friends—a few white, most black—and studied strangers with heavy-lidded, disdainful eyes. Raylene was, Feena observed from the sidelines, one of the most popular girls in school.

Which meant, of course, that Feena would have little to do with her. Feena already knew that. Although this school was bigger, more forgiving than her old one, it would require a miracle on the order of a Cinderella makeover to beam her into the privileged realm where people called you Girlfriend, sought out your opinion, copied what you wore. In fact, except for the few glimpses she had of Raylene, the otherness of her confidence, her laughter, Feena accepted her bit part and never so much as wished for a starring role.

For several weeks, then, she made her quiet way to and from classes, began to relax, to feel easy, if somewhat lonely, at her new school. She made several friends—a shy girl from History 1 who dotted every *i* in her notes with a heart, and a funny girl with glasses and a thick accent Feena couldn't place—people to sit beside in the cafeteria, to pair up with in gym. All in all, she counted herself fortunate. Until the day she discovered Raylene's secret.

"Can't you chill your sorry butts one second." Raylene was juggling books, talking over her shoulder to two girls as she headed toward her locker. "Mr. Norman and his quadratic equations can wait on us." Feena, late for her own class, was pinned to the wall as Raylene rushed by. How she admired the sophisticated, bitchy sound of the girl's words. And the lazy Southern drawl that went with them.

"What's a square root ever done for you anyhow?" Still, Raylene seemed to be in a hurry, jamming everything into the locker at once—backpack, books, papers, purse, Walkman. Of course, it didn't work, and before she could slam the door shut, most of her things clattered to the floor, bouncing and rolling toward Feena, whose sneaker toe broke the Walkman's fall.

Acting on instinct, treating Raylene as if she were nobody special, anybody at all, Feena stooped down to help. "Here," she said, handing back a spiral and an Earth Sciences text. That was when she saw it, a small book that had slipped out from the stack, a book with a familiar title: *Jane Eyre*.

"Have you read this?" Feena couldn't keep the surprise out of her voice, heard too late how condescending the question sounded. "I mean, this is one of my favorites."

For a brief second, their eyes locked. Feena saw the mild startle, the caution of an animal that's smelled or seen something in the distance, on Raylene's normally implacable face. "No." Raylene grabbed the book from Feena, scraping the rest of her books and pens and pencils out of reach, away from the help she clearly didn't want.

"No?" Feena looked away, puzzled, penitent.

"Hey, I hate to bust your balloon and all. But this book is not one of my favorites. It's not even mine." Raylene picked up her things, stood up, then moved toward the girls who were waiting down the hall. Over her shoulder again: "I'm taking it back to the library for someone. Okay?"

"Okay." Feena watched her move, proud and graceful as a dancer, toward the hangers-on. She wore a vintage skirt with a petticoat that showed just enough from under the skirt's hem. There was a pocket watch on a chain around her waist, the kind of waist Feena had been dieting for, dreaming of, forever.

"Wait!" Feena saw it just as Raylene reached her friends. "Here." Feena ran down the hall after them. "You forgot your Walkman." She caught up, the cassette player dangling from its long neon earplugs. Next came a humiliating pantomime as she tried to disentangle herself from the Walkman. Clownlike, she twisted and untwisted the cord, then finally succeeded in freeing herself, only to watch the player separate from the cord and clatter to the floor again.

This time, the Walkman didn't survive the fall, its plastic case breaking on impact and skittering away like the two halves of an eggshell. Raylene stared at the halves, then at Feena.

"Oh, my god." Feena was on her knees in an instant. "What's the matter with me?" She gathered up the innards, the pieces of case. "I was just...I mean..." Then, as if it could somehow reassemble itself into a working unit, she handed the whole mess back to its owner.

Without acknowledging Feena's stammering, or even her existence, the slender girl accepted the smashed Walkman, glanced at it once, then shook her head. As she left with her friends, she held the plastic parts away from her body, the way people keep their distance from garbage. And sure enough, as the group passed the main office, Feena saw her drop the remains into the trash.

It was only after the others had disappeared, down another locker-lined corridor, that Feena noticed the paperback. It must have spilled from Raylene's armful and was now wedged under the bottom of a trash basket. Feena pulled it out and studied the cover. *Their Eyes Were Watching God* was the title, and underneath was a picture of a beautiful black woman with a long braid down the middle of her back, a woman who looked just like Raylene.

For a moment, Feena considered chasing after the girls, returning the book. But then she remembered Raylene's expression, the look of contempt she'd leveled at the broken Walkman. Rather than risk another dose of humiliation, Feena tucked the little book in with her own things and walked in the other direction down the hall.

All through next period, she did instant replays in her head. While the rest of English class was analyzing *Macbeth,* Feena was dissecting her run-in with Raylene: If only she hadn't been late to class. If only she hadn't tried to help. If only she'd ignored the book Raylene had dropped.

Had Raylene lied about *Jane Eyre*? Feena couldn't remember seeing a library number on the dog-eared paperback. But she did remember the brief furtive look in Raylene's eyes. Was that brassy in-your-face girl ashamed of being smart? Of reading? Of being like Feena?

Of course she was, Feena realized. Who in their right mind wouldn't be? Who would trade useless book chat (about a book that wasn't even on the English reading list) for being one of the chosen ones? Second-best swimmer in school. Secretary of the student council. Resident Amazon. If she herself were any of these, Feena decided, she would have lied, too. But she knew, as surely as she knew she could never get a slip to hang that way, or move like music down the hall, that she and Raylene would never travel in the same circles. Never be friends. Not even acquaintances, now that Feena had confirmed her own status as a spastic moron. Why hadn't she held on to that Walkman? Why hadn't she been able to say she was sorry?

She *was* sorry, of course. Sorry she'd broken the Walkman. Sorry she had freckles and small breasts. Sorry she had a mother whose idea of togetherness was pressing the pause button on the remote. Sorry she lived in a laughable house that ruled out sleepovers and guests of any kind.

Even though the girl from history kept asking her over after school, Feena wouldn't go because she couldn't bear to invite anyone to the Pizza Hut. She'd made all sorts of twisted excuses: they hadn't finished unpacking, her mother was sick, the house was being painted. Or fumigated. Or something. Finally, the girl stopped asking.

Which was why every day now Feena found herself doing the same thing after school she'd done all summer—reading. Sometimes she lay on the floor under the air conditioner in her bedroom; sometimes she took her book across the highway to the shady carcass of an abandoned restaurant, complete with a gutless kitchen stove and two booths you could sort of sit in if you avoided the curling edges of their slashed plastic seats. But mostly she just stayed in the Chevy and let the air run.

That's where she headed as soon as *Macbeth* had been picked apart and eighth period ended. Still nursing her embarrassment, she decided to skip the play that had been assigned for the next day and read Raylene's book instead. The author was a black woman; Feena saw her posed on the back cover in a flapper hat and beads. *A powerful love story,* it said under the photo. *One of the finest novels of all time.*

The heat built up behind the car's window, even with the AC roaring and sputtering. Stretched across the front seat, both vents aimed at her face, Feena went into the trance she always did when she read. Soon she was lost. To the heat, to the drone, to everything but Janie Woods, the lonely heroine:

> *So the beginning of this was a woman and she had come back from burying the dead. Not the dead of sick and ailing with friends at the pillow and the feet. She had come back from the sodden and the bloated; the sudden dead, their eyes flung wide open in judgment.*

This Janie, Feena saw right away, was no frightened Jane Eyre. She was regal and proud and strong. She walked right into town by herself, with the whole neighborhood gossiping and staring.

> *The men noticed her firm buttocks like she had grape fruits in her hip pockets; the great rope of black hair swinging to her waist and unraveling in the wind like a plume . . .*

No, nothing like poor stammering Jane—or Feena, for that matter. Janie wore her brave heart for everyone to see. Graceful and serene, she moved down the street, parading past a porch full of gawkers and busybodies, just like Raylene striding down the halls at school.

...nobody moved, nobody spoke, nobody even thought to swallow spit until after her gate slammed behind her.

Feena was still living the book's dream, still sitting with Janie on the stoop of her old house, listening to her hard story, when the woman and the little boy named Christopher came back to Ryder's. Feena had no idea how long they'd been there before she looked up from the book and recognized the child. Not only because he still wore the same filthy T-shirt she'd seen him in last time, not only because he was still being yelled at by this foul-tempered mother, but because, she thought, she would have known him anywhere. Would have singled out that white hair, those solemn eyes, even if it had been years instead of weeks since she'd seen him.

This afternoon was different, though. The play Christopher and his mother acted out today had a new uglier script. The toddler's mother was no longer slapping him; she was kicking. By the time Feena had turned off the car's engine, slipped the key into the pocket of her shorts, and run to the gate, the woman was standing over him, screaming.

"Don't you dare get up!" She shoved a sneakered foot into Christopher's leg when he tried to raise himself from the asphalt. He crumpled like a rag doll. "I told you to stay right there and think about how rude you was." Again he attempted to stand, and again she tripped him back into a sitting position on the pavement.

As Feena rushed toward them, she glanced around the park. She didn't see Mr. Milakowski anywhere. The only adult she spotted was the mother of a small unsmiling girl who rode by herself in one of the fire engines. The woman scowled disapprovingly at Christopher's mother, but when her daughter pointed, showing interest in the proceedings, she hoisted the child from the ride, grabbed her by the hand, and rushed off, as if she were hustling them away from an accident.

"You keep mouthing off, you going to be pretty sorry." The little boy was crying steadily now, scrambling to his feet but being knocked down again and again. It was as if his brain hadn't gotten the message that it would hurt less to stop trying to get up. "Okay, Mister. See how you like it when you got no audience."

Feena wished there were somebody—anybody—else around. She almost ran after the other mother and her little girl, but then she heard a car start up in the parking lot and knew it was too late. Knew she was the only one left, Christopher's last hope. She remembered, as if it were a dream, running, pushing her way through a forest of adults. *Christy? Where's Christy?* Trembling with an old, speechless indignation, she had no idea what she would say, how she would stop the angry woman. All she thought about, all she felt was the forward motion, the race to save him.

four

.

.

.

Righteous, angry words formed themselves in Feena's head as the woman pushed past her. *I hope your little boy held up a bank or murdered someone, lady.* But now, just as she had the last time, Christopher's mother was sailing off, her back to them. *Unless he has, you've got no right to treat a baby like that.* But before Feena could run after her, the woman turned and headed, thick legs churning purposefully, for the parking lot.

Christopher's mother didn't stop the way she had last time. She didn't change her mind and come marching back to claim her son like so much forgotten baggage. Feena and the baby watched her get into a battered, beige convertible. They watched her start the car, and together, in silence, they watched her drive away.

When Feena turned to the little boy, he was still staring at the spot where the car had been. Not knowing what else to do, she knelt down and held out her hand. He took it. "Don't worry," she said, afraid he might startle, might run away. "Everything will be okay."

He turned his solemn gaze on her now, as if deciding whether or not to overlook the ridiculous promise she'd just made. His eyes were so blue, so like a painting or a photograph, Feena was glad of the brown stain—juice or ice cream or who knew what—that ran from the side of his mouth almost to his right ear. It made him real. "Mama," he said, regarding her with mild curiosity.

"Your mama's gone," she told him. Then, because this wasn't what he wanted to hear, she added quickly, "Want to wait for her with me?"

He didn't nod, but he didn't let go her hand, either. And when she picked him up, when his sticky fingers closed around her neck, it felt as if he'd always perched there, solid and warm and only a little heavy in her arms. They might have waited for his mother where they stood, might have toughed it out, faithfully scanning the parking lot for her car. But it was too hot, Feena reasoned, studying the empty, sun-beaten rides, the stretch of gooey asphalt. It was too hot, and they'd be more comfortable in the shade across the highway, where they could stay cool and still keep an eye out for the tan Buick.

They crossed the street quickly and stood for a while on the other side. Then Feena remembered the can of orange soda she'd left in the old restaurant. They'd waited only a few minutes, but suddenly that seemed long enough. "Christy," she said, shifting his weight against her hip, "want to see an old castle? It's got a whole garden growing right up through the floor."

She didn't wait for an answer, just looked one more time at the parking lot, then headed down the highway. She didn't stop until they'd reached the pile of fallen timbers under a broken neon sign that hadn't flashed in years. LER'S, was all that was left on the sign's first line; AUNT, it announced on the second. Sometimes, here by herself, she'd made a game of guessing what the full name of the restaurant had been. But now, the only thing she cared about was ducking into the shade.

She brushed aside a pile of dried palm fronds and jagged glass, moving them with her toe as she stepped through what had once been a door. "Isn't this great?" she asked in a bright solicitous voice she hardly knew. "Doesn't it make a perfect hideout?"

As she set the baby down on one of the cracked vinyl booth seats, a tiny lizard the color of new grass shot between Feena's feet. Like the pink chameleons she sometimes surprised on the tile walls of the girls' room at school, the lizard made a fast break for cover, disappearing under the two-legged Formica table that had collapsed at a useless angle between the seats.

"There," she told Christopher, as if something had been settled between them. "There you are." The soda, which she'd stashed under one of the booths, wasn't exactly cold. But it was liquid, and the baby covered both her hands with his, pulling the can close, gulping it down.

"Mu," he said.

There was no more. But she didn't tell him that. Instead, she adopted a prissy maternal tone. "That's enough for now," she said. "We'll get some milk later."

"Mu," Christopher repeated, eyeing her calmly. "Want mu."

The way he looked at her! It was as if she were a goddess, a minor deity of some sort, who could supply his every need. As if she were everything good and beautiful in the world. When she picked him up again, she knew ahead of time how it would be, how he would collapse against her, yield himself completely.

"We'll have more later," she said. "Now it's time for a nap." She felt the dampness on her arm. "And a change of diapers," she added, wondering how on earth she'd manage that.

She didn't want to move him again, didn't want to risk going back to the parking lot, where the beige convertible might now be parked, waiting. She didn't want—she had to admit it now—to give Christopher back. Not yet. Not before she'd shown him, for just a little while, for a tiny slice of time no one else would miss, that things could be different.

So she stretched him out full-length on the seat, let him bat at strands of her hair, while she tugged off his jeans. After she'd slipped the sodden, smelly diaper from between his legs, she took off her own shorts. She stepped out of her underpants, folded them into a thick pad, then tucked them under his bottom. It was the only thing she could think to do. It was just what she'd done two years ago, when her period had started in the girls' room at school and she'd been too embarrassed to go to the nurse.

"There," she said again. She didn't know if it was perverted to look at him naked. Still, she couldn't help thinking that his penis reminded her of an extra finger, a tiny, misplaced digit. It wasn't like the pink wilted worms you saw on cherubs in old paintings. It was standing straight up and it was pointing right at her.

In Connecticut, most of their neighbors had been elderly, and Feena had only babysat once. For a couple with twin boys. The babies had been asleep when she got there, and were still asleep when she'd left. She'd spent the whole week before, folding a paper napkin into diapers for an old doll, reading about diaper rash and colic, feeding and burping. At first, she'd been sorry she never got a chance to put her skills to the test. But later, when girls in her class told stories about baby boys who peed all over you the minute their diapers came off, she thought maybe she hadn't missed too much.

"All fixed." She pulled the front of her underpants between Christy's legs and covered him up, then put her own shorts back on. Maybe it was the soda or the relief of being dry, but now the baby's eyes shut and his breathing slowed. "That's good," she crooned, reaching for his jeans. "Time to sleep."

She had slipped both his feet into the pants legs before she noticed the marks on his right thigh. There were seven tiny reddish circles arranged like the Big Dipper on his pale skin. Though it didn't appear to be necessary, she repeated it, her voice hushed and singsong. "Time to sleep."

When Feena was little, her father had taken her out under the night sky. "Right up there, honey. See it?" Feena had craned her neck, found the bright dots. "That's the Big Dipper. And just to this side? That's the Baby Dipper. See?"

But the constellation on Christopher's leg was different. The spots were oozing and inflamed, like poison ivy. "Somebody's been letting you walk around wet," she told him, pulling up his jeans, covering the sores. "That is some case of diaper rash, Christy."

He didn't seem to mind, though. He turned on his side in his sleep, his head on one dirty arm, the fingers of his other hand still caught in Feena's hair. Gently, she unwound each strand, then sat down beside him to think. Crickets were already thrumming in the grass around her feet, and she listened for the music coming from the amusement park. It had stopped.

There, in the quiet, it hit her: She was a kidnapper. She had snatched somebody's child! Granted, anybody would have done the same thing, wouldn't they? Nobody, she was sure, could watch what she had and not take action.

But now what? Maybe the woman with the sweet face and too much makeup was missing her baby. Feena pictured her: remorseful, tears and mascara streaming down her cheeks, driving back to Ryder's. She imagined her flushed with despair, searching the empty park, then racing to the police.

The police! If Christopher's mother had gone to the police, they'd be looking for him by now. They'd probably start at Ryder's, then fan out, the way they did in detective stories. It wouldn't be long before they'd find Feena's hiding place.

She pictured the baby, handed by a beaming police officer back to his mother; pictured the woman, relieved, sniffling. Then she saw another picture, a picture of what would happen when the two of them got home. "Who do you think you are, Mister?" Christopher's mother would yell. "Just who do you think you are, running away like that?" Then Christopher would duck his head, go into his fighter's stance, and the hitting would start.

And Feena would never see him again. Never feel his head against her shoulder. Never catch him staring at her as if she were all he needed.

She didn't wait for him to wake up. Carefully, she scooped him up, still heavy with sleep, then picked her way through the rubble to the woods behind what must have once been the restaurant's back door.

She'd heard about snakes in the South, copperheads and rattlers and black snakes, so she watched where she walked, staying just inside the line of trees that led back toward the Pizza Hut. The sweat poured off her, and heat seemed to steam out from the ferns below, the creepers overhead. When she was opposite the house, she pushed aside tall weeds and parched, tangled fronds to stare past the road to the parking lot. It was still empty.

Good. And better still, the Chevy was missing from the narrow driveway beside the Pizza Hut. If her mother hadn't left too long ago, Feena would have time to get supplies. She headed across the highway as fast as she could, trying not to jostle Christopher awake.

Why were there no police cars at Ryder's? No blockades? She wondered about the hole that was left when a little boy wasn't where he was supposed to be. Maybe, she thought, angry and relieved at once, it was too small for anyone to notice. And the anger carried her along, like the slick, dark muscle of a wave. If his mother didn't care, Feena decided, if the police didn't care, she did. If no one else heard Christy cry, if no one else saw him raise his arms to be picked up, she had.

The baby continued to sleep, snoring softly against her even after she'd maneuvered the lock, then kicked the front door wide and pushed it shut behind them. She worked her way across the shade-darkened living room, nearly tripping over an open magazine lying facedown by the couch. In her room, she laid Christopher on the bed, then hurried into the kitchen.

The shopping list was missing from under the pineapple-shaped magnet on the refrigerator. That explained why the TV was off and her mother was out. Quickly, Feena raided the shelves above the sink, dumping cans of soup, applesauce, and beef stew into a paper bag. The refrigerator, as she'd expected, was nearly empty, its metal shelves skeletal, immaculate. She found a slightly brown banana and two plums in the crisper, then sat down to write a note. *Mom.* She tried to angle her script carelessly, as if this were nothing special. *At a friend's house.* As if she were invited to all sorts of places, every day. *Back tonight,* she almost wrote but decided that sounded too specific, too intentional. *Back later. Feen.*

She stuck her note under the magnet, then went to check the bathroom for toilet paper and soap. She dropped an extra toothbrush into the bag, too, hoping she'd find a public restroom or a water fountain, where she could help Christy brush his teeth. She liked the idea of circling him with her arms, showing him how to scrub the front of his teeth up and down, the sides back and forth. "Feena, Feena," her father had sung when he taught her, "make 'em cleana. Feena, Feena, in betweena. Woosh. Woosh. Woosh."

Smiling, she tiptoed back to her room, watched the little boy sprawled peacefully on her bed. She indulged, for only a second or two, the wish that she could sleep there with him, that he belonged to her. But she knew it was time to leave, to pick him up and try to juggle the bag of food and his groggy, limp body. She was actually glad when he woke. And even more glad when she saw the expression on his face. It was as close to a smile as she'd seen him come. "Mu now?" he asked, without missing a beat.

Of course! She'd promised him more soda. She put him down and grabbed his hand, leading him back into the kitchen. She opened the refrigerator again and came out with a half-full bottle of flat Pepsi. "Okay," she told him. "Just like I said, right?"

Again he cupped his hands over hers, hugging the bottle to his chest, gulping down the fizzless cold. "Now," she said before he could ask for seconds, "we have to go." She held out her hand, and when she looked down at him, she saw it again. That half smile, like a new moon. He slipped his hand in hers and followed her, as if he always had, out the door.

five

•

•

•

She felt like a criminal, but as she took the butterfly clip out of her backpack, Feena was proud, too. Astonished that, despite the rush and confusion, her brain had been scheming, coming up with a plan. Part of her, she realized, was resourceful and independent, like Janie, Raylene's heroine.

She made a game of it now, putting the big pink clip in the baby's hair, showing him in the mirror she fished from under her books. "See how pretty you look?" she cooed. She adjusted the plastic ornament, raking back his long curls with it, reclipping it like a barrette behind his right ear. "A butterfly landed on Christy, because he's so sweet. Right?"

She kissed him on his dirty, fuzzy head, and stopped feeling clever. A wave of tenderness, of proprietary fondness, washed over her. Was this what it was like to have a child? To walk through the world assured of someone's love?

They followed the dusty path that wound from behind her house, along a dried-up creek, until they found civilization—a public library branch, a play-ground, and best of all, a small strip mall. The minute they got within sight of the playground, Christopher tugged repeatedly at her hand, little animal spurts of yearning. It was late and there were only a few children on the jungle gym, intent at demolition projects in the small round sandbox. Christopher lunged happily toward them, and she let him go, hoping his makeshift disguise would hold.

"Hi." Never very outgoing, Feena surprised herself with the tinny friendliness in her voice. She sat down on one of the benches next to a woman with a braid. "Is that your son? I hope my little sister isn't bothering him."

The woman smiled at her, open, easy. "No," she said, turning back to the playground as Christopher toddled over to a short round boy making hopeless swipes at the monkey bar. "How old?"

"What?"

"How old's your sister?"

"Oh." Feena realized the woman was making small talk. She didn't suspect a thing. For her, Christopher was a cute, towheaded little girl in jeans. And a butterfly clip! "Two." Feena watched Christopher grab the little boy's arm. "Two and a half."

"Angel's four," the woman told her.

"Angel?"

"Yep. That's his real name. Named after my grandfather." The woman flipped her braid behind her. "Anyway, Angel's four. But he loves little ones." She studied the children, proud, relaxed. "Especially girls."

They talked, the two of them, while Christopher made inroads. Soon he and Angel had appropriated the sandbox and were helping its formerly lone occupant mold and stomp paper-cup houses. It was so right, so natural, Feena grabbed her chance.

"My name's Candace." She'd always liked the impudent, breezy sound of that name. It made her feel braver, somehow, holding out her hand to this stranger, this adult.

"I'm Dale," the braided woman told her.

"Dale, do you think you could do me a big favor?" Feena stared past the playground to the strip mall. "Do you think you could watch my sister while I run and get some diapers?" She smiled at Dale, a you-know-what-it's-like apology. "We've run out."

"Why, sure," the older woman told her. "You go ahead. Your sister will be fine right here." She stood up just as Feena walked away. "Wait, honey. What's her name?"

"Chris—" It was too late, she'd already said it, too late to call it back. "Christina," she said, furious at herself. "It's Christina."

The CVS was crowded with after-work shoppers. Despite her success with Dale, Feena was afraid to meet their eyes. What if they'd heard it on their radios? What if they all knew about the kidnapping? A police officer in plain clothes might be watching the diaper section right now. She might walk straight into a trap if she hesitated, stood too long deciding on brands. She wasn't worried for herself so much. But the thought of returning Christy to his mother, of watching the held-back smile she'd seen bloom on his face fade and disappear into that patient, hopeless stare, was more than she could bear.

Feeling shy, vulnerable under the fluorescent lights, she watched from a distance while other women shopped for canned formula and baby food. After two of them chose the diapers with a somersaulting baby on the wrapper, she did, too. Quickly, she darted toward the shelves, plucked up a package, then headed for the brushes and combs.

This was an easier decision. She simply chose what she would have liked when she was little, when she loved to wear ponytail wraps with fluffy pompoms on the ends. She used to sit quietly, as close to purring as a human can come, while her mother brushed and brushed her hair. Just the two of them—no daddy, no baby, no TV. Her mother beside her, humming, stopping sometimes to say, "Gorgeous, Feen. You've got gorgeous hair."

She picked a card of pink pompoms and a card of speckled blue and white ones before she saw the stuffed rabbit. It was in the next aisle over, and it was wearing a dress that would just fit Christopher. The closer she got, the better it looked. The bunny, made of soft, tan plush, was nearly as big as Christy himself. Without its patchwork jumper, it would make a perfect toy. She picked it up, hoping she could afford it, noting the dress's Velcro fasteners that would make it easy to slip onto a wiggler.

Seven ninety-five! She knew, of course, if she'd stopped to look at something like this back in Connecticut, her friend Denise would have told her that children in China had been forced to work long hours putting lace on the jumper pockets, pink lining in the rabbit's ears. But now all Feena felt was relief that CVS had probably bought hundreds, thousands of bunnies—

enough to bring the price down to her level. Enough to give Christy a new disguise and something to cuddle. She couldn't put faces on the rows of poor hungry children she'd conjured up. So she left them sitting there, their machines clattering more and more faintly as she hurried to the checkout counter.

The line snaked all the way to the pharmacy, so when Feena stepped behind the last person, she had plenty of time to torment herself with what-ifs. What if Christy got sick? She studied the shelves: There were bottles of aspirin, bottles of decongestants, boxes of antihistamines. What if he needed a doctor? The back of one bottle listed one dose for children under one hundred pounds, another for children under fifty. NOT TO BE ADMINISTERED TO CHILDREN WITH FLU SYMPTOMS, one label warned. NOT TO BE TAKEN WITH ORAL ANTIBIOTICS OR ANTI-INFLAMMATORY MEDICATIONS, another advised. What if she made a mistake? Or missed a symptom, a sign? What if Christy slipped away like her brother had? *"Sometimes babies stop breathing and no one knows why."* She remembered her mother's face, stiff as a mask, a scary new voice seeping out from it. *"Every once in a while, a baby dies, too."*

"These for you?"

Feena suddenly found herself at the head of the line, face-to-face with one of the last people she wanted to see.

"I said, are these for you?" Raylene Watson picked up the package of diapers, ran them expertly over the scanner.

"What are *you* doing here?" It was somehow ironic, preposterous to see Raylene's placid smile, her gleaming crown of cornrows above the red CVS smock and glassy-faced nametag. HELLO, the tag announced, MY NAME IS RAY. Embarrassed by her own wrinkled tee, and by the diapers and pompoms, Feena glanced instinctively toward the store window, searched the playground. But it was too far away to pick out anyone, to reassure herself that Christy was still there. "I mean, I didn't know you worked here."

"Sorry I didn't check with you first," Raylene told her, still smiling—was that grin pasted to her face?—reaching for the dressed-up rabbit. "How old's your little sister?" The first time over, the rabbit's dress caught on a corner of the scanner. Raylene grabbed the toy by its neck and dragged it across again.

"What?"

"Your baby sister," Raylene repeated, waving the pompoms. "How old is she?"

Lord, why did everyone want to know kids' ages? It was as if a number gave them a handle, a way in; it was the question of the hour. "Two and a half." Feena fumbled in her backpack for the week's lunch money. While the older girl bagged what she'd bought, Feena offered up a little prayer of thanksgiving that the woman in the cafeteria at school had refused to take her money. "Got to have a lunch form," she'd told Feena sternly. "Can't take that without no form." But Feena had forgotten the form, forgotten even to have her mother sign it.

As she counted out the change, Feena forced herself not to look out the window, to watch instead, as if it were open-heart surgery, Raylene's slender hands widening the mouth of a plastic bag, dropping in the toy and the diapers. "Well," Feena said when there was nothing else to say. She glanced at the man in line behind her as if he were waiting impatiently for his turn at the register, instead of standing impassively staring at a display of batteries and miniature flashlights. "I'll see you in school."

Raylene didn't stop smiling, didn't even nod. "Sure," she said, turning to the battery man. "Welcome to CVS," she told him in a voice that sounded like an answering machine. "Did you find everything you need today?"

Feena propped her bag under one arm and tried to walk casually toward the door. Once outside, though, she streaked back to the park, to Dale on the bench and Christopher in the sandbox. He was covered, she could see even before she lifted him up and felt it, with a layer of damp gritty sand. "Thanks so much," she told Dale.

"Thanks a lot." She wished she'd gotten some candy for the other little boy, but seeing Raylene had frozen her brain.

Christopher pulled away when she held out her hand, refused to give up his freedom. She wondered whether he would cry if she simply plucked him up and carried him off.

"Oh, that's okay. They were real good together," Dale told her. "We got to get home, though. Maybe we'll see you tomorrow?" She joined Feena at the sandbox, and Feena watched gratefully as first Angel, then Christopher, in imitation, held up their hands and let themselves be lifted out of the sandbox.

It was only when they'd left the playground and were heading toward the dense growth along the highway that Feena remembered the book she'd forgotten to hand over to Raylene. And then the milk she'd meant to buy. "Damn!" She said it out loud, and Christopher turned his head toward her, searched her face as if looking for storm signals. She was instantly sorry she'd raised her voice, sorry she'd put him on alert, his whole body stiffened into a holding pattern.

"We forgot to get milk," she explained to him. "You need to drink milk and brush your teeth before bed," she added, not knowing where she'd heard this new rule, or why it seemed so important. But it was. So they edged their way back toward the Texaco station she'd seen by the mall.

It had restrooms and a Quick Mart, and the boy behind the counter didn't even glance up from the pocket video game in his lap when Feena and the baby walked in. He didn't look old enough to be selling cigarettes and beer, and he certainly wasn't interested in customers. Feena had time to study the two large racks of newspapers and magazines in front of the counter. She tried to read the headlines in the local paper, to get close enough without distracting the boy. She had dreaded what she might find splashed across the front page—TEEN SWIPES TODDLER or COPS CONFOUNDED BY KIDNAPPING. But instead, in the same family-size type she'd fantasized, she read: DOLPHINS TAKE DIVE IN THIRD.

First, she felt relief, and then she felt foolish. It couldn't be in the papers yet. Even if the sweet-faced woman had gone to the police right away, only television and radio would have the story so early.

Television! She thought of her mother, certainly home by now, glued to the Sony shrine. She imagined Lenore, swept up in her shows, suddenly ejected from the dream by a fast switch to the news desk and a paper-shuffling anchor: "We interrupt our regular programming for up-to-the-minute coverage of one of Florida's most despicable crimes. Early this afternoon..."

Foolish again, she told herself. This wasn't the Lindbergh kidnapping, after all. She still remembered the way the history teacher at her old school had actually gotten tears in his eyes when he described how the

Lindberghs had begged the kidnapper to return their baby. Begged and begged, without knowing that it was too late, that the little boy was already dead, discarded like so much garbage in the woods a few miles from his house.

But Christopher wasn't dead. And his mother wasn't famous. What was more, she might not have reported him missing. Feena remembered those formidable arms, their relentless swipes at Christy's head and shoulders. Why, she might have driven off and not come back. Might be glad to be rid of him. And even if she wasn't, how would she explain to the police that she'd left him at Ryder's? Abandoned him, that's what she'd done. Feena hadn't kidnapped Christy, she'd *found* him, that was all. Lost and found.

The boy at the counter still hadn't looked their way. Feeling braver now, and much more self-righteous, Feena led the baby between the Tastykakes and the chips to the large green door at the back of the store. There was no stick person painted on the front, no upside-down-triangle skirt or long thick pants to tell them whether the bathroom was for women or men. But Feena didn't care. All she knew was how good it felt, how safe, once she'd slid the lock closed behind them.

six

.

.

.

If Christopher had ever brushed his teeth, he seemed to have forgotten all about it. As Feena pulled the toothbrush out of the bag from home, he stared as if he'd never seen anything like it before. Tentatively, he touched its bristles, then pulled his fingers back quickly. He was willing enough, though, to perch on the edge of the sink and peer into the dusty mirror while Feena demonstrated her preferred brushing technique.

"Cwiss," he said, delighted with the sandy face he saw in front of him. "Cwiss, Cwiss, Cwiss," he chanted rhythmically until Feena realized he'd been watching himself, not her. "Cwiss, Cwiss, Cwiss," he repeated as she squeezed the toothpaste onto the brush, determined to do the job for him. "Cwiss, Cwiss, Cw—" He tried to keep going, even with the brush in his mouth.

"If you think you look good now," she told him when she'd finished and had rinsed out the brush, "wait till you see yourself cleaned up." She wet a paper towel and rubbed it over his filthy cheeks, inside the folds of his neck. "Now," she said, presenting him to the mirror again. "Who's that?"

"Cwiss?" he asked, checking with her rather than his reflection.

"The *new-and-improved* Chris," she said, tossing the towel into the trash and turning his head back to the glass. "Say hello to the clean and totally adorable Chris."

"Wo," he told himself, obligingly. "Wo, Cwiss."

"Is there anyone cuter in the whole world?" she asked, shaking her head. He shook his right along with her.

"How cute are you, Chris?" she said, setting him down now, opening her arms across the damp, ammonia smell of the room. "Soooooooooo cute." When he opened his own arms, she couldn't help picking him up again, nuzzling his neck, kissing the soft, still-damp skin behind his ears. "Now," she told him, "milk and bed."

But that meant opening the door. Going back into the world, where good people, law-abiding citizens, would think what she had done was wrong. Would want to take Christy away and give him back to his mother. Feena gripped his hand and wished they could leave without seeing the clerk. Mercifully, he was still engrossed in the badly lit figures on his Gameboy, and they slipped past him to the baby food. Feena kept hold of Christopher, chose a squat glass jar containing alarmingly yellow Easy Chew Peaches. She was sure he was old enough for regular food, but it would be good to have, just in case. When they reached the dairy cooler, she lifted out a quart of milk, not thinking about how they'd keep it refrigerated.

They were headed for the counter when she saw the face on the carton. It wasn't Christy's, she knew that; the carton must have been printed weeks ago. But the eyes were the same, and the nimbus of hair, like spun glass, above the small features, the uncertain smile. HELP FAIRHILL DAIRIES FIND THIS CHILD, it said in large letters under the black-and-white photo. Then, beneath those, in smaller type, were the facts. NAME: *Lester Milton Dailey.* DATE BORN: *August 12, 1998.* DATE MISSING: *March 21, 2002.* LAST SEEN: *Oak Park, Illinois.* At the bottom of the carton was an 800 number.

Feena felt teary, indignant, as she studied the picture. *Who would name a baby Lester, anyway?* She looked at the little boy's half-closed eyes, his wary smile. *They probably didn't even love him. They obviously hadn't cared how the flashbulb frightened him when they took this picture.*

Christy reached up, tried to lower her arm, take the carton from her. "Me carry," he urged. "Me carry mik."

Maybe there was no "they." Maybe the boy's father had left, and there was just the baby and his mother. Was she waiting, just out of the picture's frame? Was she a careless, angry mother who didn't take care of him, who didn't deserve a second chance?

As if it were burning her hands, Feena yanked the milk away and dropped it back in the dairy case. *Being a lousy mother wasn't like making a mistake on a computer, after all. You couldn't just press the delete key and make everything all right again.*

"We'll get little ones instead," she said, plucking up a pint carton and giving another to Christopher to carry. *Would Christy's face be on next week's cartons? Did his mother have a picture of him—some sloppy, phony Kodak moment that would make people sure she loved him?* "That's it," she soothed, closing his tiny fingers around the milk, herding him back toward the counter. "That's my helper."

The boy was still bent over his Gameboy. Barely looking at them, he extended one arm and spread his palm while he continued to detonate tiny star shapes on the gray screen. Once Feena had fished some change from her pocket, though, and led Christy out of the store, things got harder.

She considered going back to the abandoned restaurant, but it was too far from the house, and it had no doors that shut, no way to make sure he'd stay where she left him. She needed to put him to sleep where she could hear him if he woke and cried, somewhere safe and close.

If only she could take him home, tell Lenore what had happened. For an instant, a syrupy millisecond, Feena imagined herself curled up with Christy in her own bed. But then she pictured the long walk they'd have to take to get there, Lenore looking at them over the remote. Her mother would never understand, Feena was sure of it. Not even if she turned off the TV long enough to listen.

That was when it occurred to her that the cleverest criminals often did exactly what the police were certain they wouldn't do. They returned to the scene of the crime. Isn't that how the "perps" on her mother's favorite detective series always made fools of an entire city—until, of course, the heavy, wisecracking star of the show figured things out?

So she retraced her steps, headed toward the Pizza Hut, then behind it, and into the parking lot of Ryder's. The place was deserted—no cars, no lights except for the neon *S* in Ryder's, which sputtered and winked in the twilight like a giant firefly. "Can't turn it off," Mr. Milakowski always complained. "Why do I need that,

I'm asking? I close at five, I open at ten. For what do I need an *S* in the sky?"

Even though it was getting dark, Feena kept them in the cover of the rides and the small sheds that housed their motors, edging cautiously toward the miniature golf course. She knew where Mr. Milakowski kept the key, and she knew from the way Christopher's eyes lit up when he saw the little house with its red roof and the giraffe painted on the door that she'd found just the right place for him to sleep.

She wasn't prepared, though, for the steam bath inside. There was, naturally enough, no reason for the booth to be air-conditioned, since it was designed for handing out golf clubs, not taking up residence. Still, she felt a momentary despair when the baby, just as any sane and sensible adult would have done, tried to run back outside.

"Wait, Christy," she told him, putting the two bags down, grabbing him around the waist. "This is going to be fun." She propped open one of the metal flaps, then held him up to look through it. "See?" she said. "We've got our own little house, just you and me." She opened the flap on the other side, and things began to cool off. "You and me and Lady Macbeth." She pulled the huge boneless bunny out of the bag and sat with it on the concrete floor.

Christopher stared, fascinated, at the rabbit but didn't try to touch it. He approached slowly, as if he thought he might startle it, then sat down across from Feena. "Lord Christopher," she said, holding the rabbit's paw, touching it to Christy's hand, "meet Lady Macbeth, the star of English 10A." She folded the rabbit's soft middle into a deep bow.

"It be-ith an honor," she squeaked for the toy, "to meet so fair a prince. Not all the perfumes in Arabia could smell as sweet," she added, snuffling Lady Macbeth's nose into Christy's cheek, pushing harder and harder until he toppled, giggling, to the floor.

While he played with his new toy, Feena sneaked a look outside, then, satisfied there was no one around, laid out the banana and plums. Surer of himself now, Christy grabbed the banana and mashed its end into the rabbit's mouth.

"I think Lady Macbeth is going to have milk instead," she told him, peeling the fruit and breaking it into pieces. He downed it in seconds, then watched intently while she tried to open a can of beef stew. She'd forgotten a can opener, but he sat patiently, betrayed only by a trembly, chewing motion of his lips, as Feena banged and pounded the can against the counter where the clubs were tucked into their long, vertical nests. *WHAM. WHAM.*

She succeeded only in denting the can and making far too much noise. Finally, she fished out the jar of peaches instead, twisted it open, and fed him with an old plastic spoon she found in the drawer with the pencils and scorecards. *"Mmmm,"* she said, as he devoured each spoonful. *"Mmmm."* Though he seemed to need no encouragement at all, seemed, in fact, to be starving.

After he'd drunk both cartons of milk—sharing make-believe sips with Lady Macbeth—and finished off the applesauce as well, Feena made him a bed out of her sweater and the paper bags. "Time for a story," she announced. "No," she said each time his head popped up. "Not until you're lying down."

She ended, of course, lying beside him; he held the rabbit and she held him. Through the open flap above them, the neon *S* blinked on and off, on and off. "This story," Feena said, "is about a young girl who worked for a mysterious stranger, a man she never saw—" She stopped, realizing that Jane Eyre's adventures at Thornfield might not be the stuff little boys dreamed of. On similar grounds, she rejected *Rebecca* and most of her old favorites. Beside her, Christopher clutched Lady Macbeth with one hand, wrapping the other through her hair. Even holding tight, though, he seemed worried, restless.

"What would you like to hear a story about?" she asked. "How about the three bears?" Christy shook his head.

"A brave little pig?" She thought of *Charlotte's Web,* tried desperately to resurrect the plot. But Christy shook his head again.

"Okay. What about a rabbit like Lady Macbeth?" More head shaking. Feena was beginning to think the head shaking was a game—to wonder if he even knew what it meant—when Christopher suddenly released her hair and pointed toward the slice of sky showing through the tin flap. "Nake," he said. "Want nake."

Feena looked where he pointed. "Nake," she repeated to herself, and then she understood. She thought for a minute, then began again. "This story," she told him, "is about that whirly, curly snake in the sky."

"Nake!" Christopher said, reaching for the sinuous, winking *S*. "Wo, nake!"

"Hello, snake," Feena repeated after him. She turned to Christy, who was closing and unclosing his pincer fingers, straining toward the sky.

"Nake," he said. "Want nake. Want pay nake."

"That snake's too high, Christy," she told him. "We can't play with him. But I can tell you his story, okay?"

Christopher nodded, settling against her. She told him that the snake's name was Sylvester and that he'd once been a normal snake, a snake who lived on the ground in a nice, cozy hole behind a rock.

"Wock," Christopher echoed, sleepily.

"That's right." Feena talked on, the story unfolding, to her surprise, practically as fast as she could tell it, like a flower in one of those stop-action nature films. It all started, she said, when Sylvester bit the toe of a dragon, a purple dragon with yellow spots. A purple, fire-breathing dragon, who didn't look where he was going and nearly stepped on Sylvester, but it didn't matter who was right and who was wrong; all that mattered was who was big and who was little, so Sylvester ended up being kicked way, way up in the sky.

"Up," Christopher recited in a dreamy singsong. "Nake, up."

"Yes," said Feena. "And at first, Sylvester didn't like it up there at all. But soon he made friends with a little fat star that got caught on one of his curls. And then he found out the stars had a shining school and that he could take lessons there. Well, pretty soon, what do you think happened?"

But Christopher didn't speculate. He had fallen asleep, his head collapsed against the giant rabbit, one arm laid carelessly across Feena's shoulder. Slowly, holding her breath, Feena inched her way out from under him until she was standing, fumbling in the shadows for the key. It was only then she realized she'd forgotten to use the new diapers, hoped he was tired enough to sleep until she could sneak out in the morning after her mother left for work.

If he didn't sleep through, if he woke in the middle of the night, scared and alone, she would hear him. She'd sleep without an air conditioner, leave her window open. And nothing, nothing would keep her from going to him if he needed her. She didn't dare kiss him for fear she'd wake him, but she stood still in the dark, watching the play of the light on his features. "Good night, Christy," she whispered before she shut the door. "Sleep tight."

Lenore was sitting in the cool dark. Only the TV was lit, only the TV talked. Feena had nearly reached her bedroom when her mother half turned from the set. "Have a good time?" she asked.

"It was okay." *Relax. Not too hot and not too cold.*

"New friend?"

"Sort of." *Did they interrupt movies for kidnappings? Would her mother have listened, or would she have used the extra minutes to get a snack, another drink?* "What're you watching?"

"Oh, it's just an old thing I've seen a billion times." Lenore stood up, turned her back on the television. "I'm glad you had a good time, honey. If you're hungry, I got Chinese."

Feena's insides were turning over like a stalled engine, but she was even more worried than she was hungry. "Anything special on TV? Any news?"

"News!" Lenore gave one of her disparaging snort-laughs, picked up her glass, and followed Feena into the kitchen. "I get enough tragedy at work, baby. I don't need extra doses on CNN."

Good. So far, so good. "Have you eaten, Mom?" *Quickly, before she sits down, before she starts pumping.*

"'Cause if you have, I think I'll just take some fried rice in my room, okay? I've got a ton of work."

Her mother actually looked disappointed, like someone throwing a surprise party nobody wanted. Her smile, under those mascara-ringed eyes, was forced, too quick. "Sure," she said, sitting heavily at the tiny table by the fridge. "Sure, go ahead. I'll just freshen this up." She lifted a vodka bottle over the forest of white cartons, some closed, some with their flaps wide, smeared with brown sauce. "Try the pork." She nodded toward the biggest carton. "It's got pineapple mixed in."

"You bought a lot." Feena studied the food, the two places set at the table, each with one of the flamingo glasses Lenore had bought as a joke the day they moved in. The glasses had a plastic reservoir around the outside, so when you held them up to drink, a flurry of pink birds and metal confetti rushed toward your mouth.

Lenore, too, glanced at the table, its abundant disarray. "Yeah, well..." She sounded almost embarrassed. "I didn't know you weren't coming home."

Feena dumped pork and fried rice onto a plate, picked up some silverware, and headed to her room. "Sorry, Mom," she said, although it didn't make her feel a whole lot better. They usually ate on paper plates by the light of her mother's shows. "It's just, you know. It's a new school. There's lots of stuff to catch up on."

"Yeah, well...," Lenore repeated, not looking at Feena, not focused on much of anything so far as Feena could tell.

Minutes later, though, when she'd closed her door, opened the window, and moved the tiny pots of African violets lined up along her air conditioner—when she'd assured herself that she could see the golf booth from both a standing and a sitting position, that she could hear Christopher if he cried out—Feena's mood lifted.

The rich, heady smell of the pork, so different from the barbecued ribs she and Lenore had eaten at the fast-food stops on their endless drive south, made her feel adventurous. The soy sauce and the bits of pineapple lent a tingly sweetness to every bite. Such sweetness that as she ate, there were times, for a few seconds at least, when she forgot her life had changed, that only yards away, Christopher was waiting.

seven

•

•

•

Feena slept fitfully, only a hint of air coming through her window, the sticky plate on the floor beside her bed. In her dreams, Christy cried out again and again. Over and over she woke, peering anxiously into the night, hearing nothing but the whir of her mother's air conditioner, the faint hum from the late-night trucks that still used the highway, and the electronic crackle of the sputtering *S* just outside the golf booth.

She'd set her alarm to go off a half-hour before her mother woke for work. But she was up a full hour and a half before that, scanning the fuzzy half dawn, then creeping into the kitchen. She was determined to do better this time, to remember things like a can opener and spoons and knives. Another note, this one a bit more detailed, aimed at warding off more mother-daughter dinners.

Had to leave early—BIG TEST! Might be late again. Don't make dinner. Light. Keep it light. *XOX, Feen.*

Once outside, she sneaked to the booth, bent her head under a flap, and looked inside. Christopher lay just where she'd left him, except that the rabbit had somehow been jettisoned and was sprawled, nose down, at his feet. She took the key from its hiding place under the roof and opened the door as quietly as she could.

She had hoped to watch him sleep, just for a few minutes. But it was no good; the second she moved inside, he turned toward the door, kicked his still-sneakered feet (how could she have forgotten to take off his shoes?), and sat up, rubbing his eyes with his fists.

Instinctively, Feena knew he needed to see her face first, not the clubs or the counter or the strange place where he'd fallen asleep. Stooping down, she grabbed his hands, pulled them apart, and stared, smiling, into his half-closed eyes. "Good morning, Mister Sleepyhead," she told him.

The smile she got back, a dazzled, devoted grin, was worth the whole sleepless night. His first words, though, were a problem. "Mu," he said. "Mu mik."

"You drank all the milk last night," she said. "But don't worry"—rolling him down, shimmying his jeans off, reaching for the box of diapers—"we're going out to eat. Just you and me. Okay?"

"'Kay," he agreed, letting himself be changed, wriggling only a little, staring around the narrow room, then like a swimmer stroking for shore, finding her face again. The diapers were hard to manage, the tapes kept unsticking, and Feena pulled them so tight that they nearly met at his tiny waist.

"We're going to play dress-up today," she announced when she'd finished. She took the bunny jumper out of the CVS bag, slipped it on over his tee, and fastened the Velcro while he was still studying the lace border on the hem. "Isn't it pretty?" she asked, guiding his hand so he could feel a soft velvet square in the patchwork. "And it goes perfectly with these."

It was less easy dividing his hair into ponytails and wrapping them with the pompoms. He twisted and chattered the whole time, so that Feena, in her hurry, tied one pompom snugly behind his left ear, the other several inches higher behind the right. When she stood back to study him, she laughed. She wanted to start over, but he was much too excited. And hungry.

She stuffed the leftover plums into her backpack, closed the booth's flaps, then led him outside and locked the door. The air was almost cool at this hour, a reprieve from the swampy furnace that would start up when the turquoise and purple streaks on the horizon gave way to the full-risen sun. They moved quickly, heading for the gas station to buy milk and check the morning headlines.

The video-game fan from yesterday had been replaced by a very large woman with frosted hair and a frown line. She looked up as soon as Feena and Christy walked into the store. "Hep ya?"

Feena tightened her grip on the baby and calculated the distance to the back of the store. "We just need some milk," she said. She didn't move, though, giving the woman time to turn away, busy herself with something so they could scan the morning papers in the rack under the counter.

But the woman folded her cushiony arms and stared till Feena began to wonder if she'd called the police when she'd seen them coming. Or maybe she was a plant, waiting for backup. There were lady detectives, weren't there? At last, just when she'd decided they didn't need the milk that badly, that they would try another store later, the woman nodded her head toward the dairy case along the back wall of the store. "It's over there," she said.

Suddenly aware she'd been holding her breath, Feena felt her whole body untense. She headed down the aisle, plucking up a box of crackers and a can of tiny cocktail hot dogs on the way to the milk. Beside her, Christy eyed the shelves without touching anything, content to point out highlights as they went. "*Bwu*," he said, reaching toward the picture of a little girl in an apron with a bright blue bow in her hair. "*Bwu*," he repeated, jabbing a finger into the shirt on his own tiny chest.

Now that they weren't under surveillance, Feena took her time, studied the photograph, a smiling girl on the verge of devouring an impossibly huge iced cookie. "Right," she told Christy. "You guys are wearing the same color." She looked down at the socks she wore. "What color are these, O Wise One?"

He beamed. "*Bwu!*" Racing to a package of doughnuts: "*Bwu!*" And a carton of cottage cheese in the case: "*Bwu!*" And an ancient, limp rubber band on the floor: "*Bwu!*"

As he crouched to retrieve the rubber band, she dropped the crackers and swooped him into her arms. "*Bwu, bwu, bwu*," she said, tickling, laughing, faint with relief. "You sure like blue, don't you?"

He giggled, shifted wildly in her hold, pushing against her, walking on air like a tiny robot. Feena set him down and then retrieved the crackers. She chose four small milk cartons from the case, handing him two to carry. "There," she said. "Make yourself useful, Whiz Kid. And while we're at it, what color are the letters on your milk?"

"*Bwu!*" They said it in unison, then said it again. They chanted it all the way back down the aisle to the counter. It was only when they reached the magazine rack that Feena remembered who they were. Remembered she couldn't relax into this love. She could never relax.

But the morning's papers told her nothing. While the woman added up their purchases, Feena even picked one up and leafed through it. As if she had all the time in the world. As if she weren't really interested. There were no headlines, no articles about a missing boy. Why hadn't Christy's mother gone to the police? Wasn't it news anymore when a little boy disappeared?

She put the paper back, then took the bag the woman handed her. She paid with the last bills she had, wondering how they'd manage tomorrow on the forty-five cents in change she got back. She'd talked Christy into surrendering his milk cartons and dropping them one after the other into the bag, when the woman surprised them both.

"Here." The frown line was still there, but she wore a smile like a thin seam across the bottom of her tanned face. She held out a lollipop in a see-through wrapper. "On account of you like blue."

Christy stared at the blue pop, eyes wide. But he made no move to take it from the woman's hand.

"Here," the woman repeated, leaning down, wrapping his fingers around it. "It's for you. On account of you're such a sweet little girl."

Christy held the pop and checked in with Feena, his whole face a question mark. "I'll bet it's blueberry," she told him. "And you can have it with your milk, okay?" She turned to the woman. "Thanks," she said, meaning it. "Thanks a lot."

Outside, Feena stopped, tried to decide what to do. It was Wednesday. Her mother was at work, and in less than an hour, she was supposed to be in school. Clearly, she was going to skip, but school made her think of books. And books made her think of the library.

So that's where they ate breakfast—under a tree behind the branch library they'd seen near the park yesterday. As he had last night, Christy ate ravenously, finishing the plums, the milk, and half the crackers. By the time the library opened, his face was smeared, the heat was intense, and they were both glad to head for the basement restroom.

Afterward, cool and clean, they sat in baby-size chairs in a corner of the children's reading room. Christy, his ponytails freshly combed and tightened evenly on both sides, looked almost too precious in Lady Macbeth's jumper. For the first time, Feena wished his face were a little less appealing, his hair not quite so bright. Proud as she was of him, the last thing they needed was to call attention to themselves.

Afraid to use her library card, in case it might be traced later, she began to choose books with Christy to read right there. At first he was afraid to touch them, settled for watching her as she brought them to him one by one, opened them across his lap. But soon he learned he could take them himself—stacks of them, plucked off the low shelves and piled on a table close at hand. Big books, little books, books with red and yellow and (of course) blue covers, books with bright bold watercolor splashes for pictures, books with delicate, careful illustrations as detailed as photos. Like the fruit and the milk and crackers, Christy devoured them all.

One book in particular, though, seemed to pull him back again and again. Even when they were reading another, Feena would notice his gaze wander, stealing a look at the cover of *Mama's Music*. She couldn't understand the attraction, didn't think the book was nearly as exciting as the stories about gorillas attending grand balls, or lost dogs who grew wings, or laughing hyenas who told knock-knock jokes. But Christy clearly had his own opinion.

He begged her to read his favorite over and over, until she had it memorized. *I have a singing mama,* the first page read. *I have a singing, dancing mama,* said the second. *I have a singing, dancing, piano-playing mama,* announced the third and fourth, across a double spread. And it was here he always made her stop, pointing to the drawing of a round jolly woman who tapped her tap shoes and opened her

O-shaped mouth while she pounded away on an upright piano. "Ma," he said each time. "Ma."

Feena was mystified. Could Christy's mother possibly be a musician? She tried to picture the harsh loud-mouthed woman she'd seen at Ryder's, seated calmly at a piano, a tinkling fountain of music spilling from under her fingers. She tried, but it was so unlikely, so preposterous, she nearly laughed. "Does your mother play the piano?" she asked Christy three different times. Three different times, he tore himself from the picture, looked up at her with his new-moon smile, and nodded.

He wouldn't let the book out of his sight, persisted in moving it to the top of the pile, where he could reassure himself that it was still within reach. When it was time to go, he refused to unhand it, coming close to crying the way he had at Ryder's.

They had to pass the circulation desk on the way out, and the librarian, who had obviously spotted Christy's puckered countenance, stopped them. "Why don't I check those out for you?" she offered, not unkindly. But Feena told her they couldn't, that she'd forgotten her library card.

"I can look it up," the woman said, smiling at Christy, who hugged *Mama's Music* and two other over-size picture books to his chest. "I'd hate to lose such an eager reader."

Feena didn't like lying, knew she was pretty lousy at it. She persevered, though, on the theory that practice would make her better. "Actually, I don't think the card's on record," she said, stalling for time. "We just moved here from out of state, and I've been using my aunt's old one." She lowered her eyes. "It's expired."

"Oh." The librarian's sharp intake of breath and hushed tone suggested she understood how much such a confession must have cost Feena. "Well, why don't I just make a new one for her?"

Feena panicked. "You can't," she said, swallowing hard, thinking fast. "She died."

"I see." The librarian looked at the two of them as if they'd been orphaned. "I'm so sorry." Then she brightened. "How old are you?" she asked.

"Fourteen." It was a relief to say this one true thing.

"Then I'll just issue *you* a card. You can take the books home now and come in tomorrow with a proof of address. How would that be?"

Feena looked at Christy, crushing the three books against the lace front of his jumper as if he'd never let go. "Okay," she agreed. She sighed as the woman pulled out a form, then leaned across the desk.

"Name?"

"Jane," Feena told her, inspired. "Jane Rochester."

Before lunch, they went back to the Pizza Hut. Feena had run out of money and decided to ransack the house for loose change. She found four dollars in quarters and nickels, most of it in the pockets of her mother's cream-colored linen jacket, the one Lenore claimed went with everything. Thankfully, it didn't go with whatever she'd put on that morning.

Christy and Feena ate the little hot dogs at the playground, which was empty now, except for a large man who stood behind the swings, shading his eyes with one hand. Feena worried that he might be an undercover cop, like the ones on TV, but after a while, he turned and walked back to the mall. Probably a clerk on break, she decided, relieved, able to taste what she was eating at last.

When they'd finished lunch, Christy took a few wobbly rides on a sea horse that rocked back and forth on a giant spring, then headed for the sandbox. He sat, desultory, sifting sand through his fingers, probably missing Angel and his paper cups. Feena felt raw with the ache of watching him, wishing he could be happy, satisfied forever.

This couldn't last, she told herself. She couldn't skip school every day, and they couldn't go on hiding in bathrooms, eating out of cans. Christy needed a bed, clothes, someone keeping track of calories or vitamins or whatever you counted to make sure a meal was balanced. What did Feena know about raising children?

She knew only that she'd never experienced anything like the smug joy she felt lying next to him, the heady responsibility of his faith in her, his assumption that she would manage everything. But how could she? Why did she think she knew better than all the people who made it their business to protect kids, the people she should have turned Christy over to in the first place?

Sure, she'd be in big trouble if she took him to the police now. But she'd be in bigger trouble if she waited. When she watched him from a distance, when he wasn't pressed up against her, the small engine of his body generating that heat, she could think straight. She would spend one more night with him, she decided, give him one more special day, then she'd take him back. She'd tell the police about his mother. She'd make them believe her.

"That dress is going to be stained for life," someone said behind her.

"Huh?" Feena turned, off-guard.

"That bunny dress," Raylene Watson told her. "You'll never get that dirt out. Specially not after she's ground it in with sand." The older girl walked around the bench, pushed the picture books toward Feena, and sat down. She was wearing her CVS smock over a lemon-colored crop top and a long lavender skirt with a ruffled hem. Feena, of course, had on her standard uniform—T-shirt and shorts. "It's bound to shrink. Just about guaranteed."

"Bunny dress?" Feena repeated dumbly.

"Yeah." Raylene nodded toward Christy, who looked at them briefly, then stood up from the sand.

"Course, she *does* look a whole lot better in it than Flopsy Jo."

"Flopsy Jo?" asked Feena. It wasn't even two o'clock. What was Raylene doing out of school at this hour?

"Hmm-hmmm." Raylene smiled like she meant it this time, like she was really tickled. "That's the rabbit's name, you know. Says so right on the tag. 'Flopsy Jo, one-hundred-percent new materials. Made in Taiwan.'"

eight

•

•

•

A stolen baby in a stuffed-rabbit's dress. No money, no plan, and now someone from school to witness the whole mess. Feena felt her brain melt, then shut down. She couldn't imagine anything worse.

Christopher toddled up to them and put his hand on Raylene Watson's knee. "Mik?" he asked her. "Mu mik?"

"Sure, I can give you milk," Raylene told him, interpreting his baby talk effortlessly, hoisting him up to her lap. "But you have to come in the store and get it." She turned to Feena, who stared at her, speechless. "I'm taking over somebody's shift, so I had to cut bio. What's your excuse?"

Feena continued to stare, as though if she watched long enough, she could make either Raylene or the baby disappear.

"How come you're not in school?"

"I, uh…" It was a good question. "I…"

"You look tight in old Flopsy's dress." Raylene shifted her attention to Christy without waiting for Feena's answer. She'd lapsed into the language she used with her friends, even though she could talk like a textbook when she wanted to. Last week, they'd both been in the school office, Feena to fill out more new student forms, Raylene to see the principal. "Mr. Cantrell, sir," Raylene had told him, "my mother has made a doctor's appointment for me this afternoon. It was obviously an oversight, and she should have scheduled it later, but I wonder if I might leave early today?" Afterward, Feena had heard her cackling like a banshee all the way down the hall, as she and her crew ducked out on afternoon classes.

"Course," she told the baby now, "you won't be truly bad, less we get all that sand off. Come on with me." She stood up, held out a hand to Christy, and headed for the CVS. Wordless, hopeless, Feena stood, too, and followed after them.

Their first stop was the employees' restroom. Raylene was endlessly patient, showing Christy how to pump a thin stream of shocking-pink soap from the dispenser and how to blow-dry his hands; Feena, though, was in an agony of suspense, praying Raylene wouldn't insist on a change of diapers, ready to feign sickness, fall down in a faint, anything to prevent the discovery of Christy's gender.

She needn't have worried. Standing by the dryer, flipping the baby's hands like pancakes under the hot air, Raylene spotted the oversize clock on the wall. "I got to punch in," she announced suddenly. "You finish up with her."

But she met them outside the door a few minutes later, led them to the glass beverage case. "There's three kinds of milk—chocolate, strawberry, and just plain white. Course," she added, "I wouldn't take the white. That's older, on account of no one much chooses it."

Christy wanted chocolate, and Raylene opened a straw for him and stuck it into the carton. "I really got to get to work now," she told them. "Later." She handed the baby back to Feena, waved as she headed toward the registers.

"Say bye," Feena instructed, suddenly finding her voice. "Say bye, Raylene."

Christy, bundled again in Feena's arms, stretched from her to Raylene. "Bye, Ween," he said, waving like a trouper.

On the way out of the store, Feena checked the headlines in the pile of newspapers by the door. Nothing.

It was only the second day, she reminded herself, hurrying outside. Off balance from Raylene's goodwill, she tried to figure out why on earth the Dis Queen Herself had taken such an interest in them. She also tried to figure out their next move. School would be over soon, so they couldn't hang around the library. Maybe the restaurant?

But Christopher decided for her, lunging back toward the playground as soon as she set him down. And the minute she saw the slim, braided woman, Feena understood why. Angel, then Dale, looked up when they got closer. "Hey, Candace," Dale said, friendly, warm. "You're back."

"Not for long," Feena assured her, standing rather than joining Dale on the bench. She pictured kids pouring out of school, heading to the library. "We...we have to get home."

Dale nodded toward the sandbox. "Better tell that little sister of yours." Feena rushed after Christy, who was already halfway to Angel, who, in turn, was striding toward the sandbox.

As they got to the box and Angel stepped in and hunkered down, Feena took Christy's hand and tried to steer him away. But he pulled against her, like a dog on a leash, pointing toward Angel. "Want pay," he told her. "Want pay."

"We'll have to play later, Christy," she said, trying to make it sound like an announcement, not a suggestion. "You've got to get your nap." She looked at her watch; it was almost time for the eighth-period bell. They had to get out of there. "We can have a story, if you like." She took out one of the big books and waved it like a truce flag. "Come on. Say goodbye to Angel."

Angel glanced up at the sound of his name, only mildly interested, as Christopher tugged them closer. "She can't have it," the older boy told Feena matter-of-factly. He shifted in the sand, his chunky legs uncovering a small sand pail. "It's mine, and it's still new." He picked up the pail, ran it along the sand like a plow, leaving fat wavy tracks behind.

"Want," Christy said, yearning toward the pail, wiggling his fingers like an acquisitive spider. "Want pay."

Feena stared at the pail, which had a circus seal painted on it. Her hand tightened on Christy's, but he only tried more furiously to escape. In her mind, Feena saw another pail, a metal one, with the same seal balancing a ball on its nose. And another baby, with less hair than Christy had. A baby who looked at her with eyes lit from behind, a sun in each, shining just for her.

She glanced up toward the benches, noticed that a second woman was sitting next to Dale, talking. In the instant she turned back to the sandbox, before her brain recognized what was wrong, her body knew. Suddenly, she couldn't get enough air and her pulse was beating in her ears. When she looked up again, she understood why. The woman beside Dale, the woman smiling and smoking, was Christopher's mother.

Without explanation, before he could see the woman, Feena picked the baby up, turned, and raced toward the woods. She remembered the other baby, the one she'd given the pail to. She remembered how he'd vanished, just like that.

She ran out of breath quickly, stumbling along the dirt path that led through the woods. But it wasn't until the trees had closed around them, until the sun winked on and off behind the branches overhead, that she slowed down. It was the day she'd found the three pinecones. That was the day the baby had disappeared. She could still hear the grown-up voices, telling her how babies die in their cribs, how they stop breathing and no one knows why.

It was too late to tell whether Christopher's mother and Dale had watched them leave. All she could do was stand, sweating, and try to catch the sound of footsteps over her sharp, painful panting.

Feena held him tight, this new baby. Even when she was sure they weren't being followed, she started running again. Leaving behind all those quiet, reasonable voices. The ones who told her babies disappear and there's nothing you can do.

Christy? She was shaking when she collapsed onto the booth. The shadowy carcass of the restaurant seemed damper, more threatening than it ever had. She noticed a crumpled soda can on the steeply angled table. Was this a hangout? Did people come here all the time? Her arms and legs were stiff, as if her veins had filled with water—heavy, sloshing. *Where's Christy?*

"Don't worry," she told him, though he didn't seem to be in the least upset. Now that she'd set him down, in fact, Christopher brightened. He reached across her for a book, opening it onto her lap. He moved his hands over the painted keys of the piano in the picture. "Ma."

Feena couldn't bear the thought of Christy's mother, of her arms, her voice, her small, pretty features lost in the center of that wide face. "No," she said, too sternly. "Not now." She pushed the book away, and his eyes clouded. "Ma," he repeated. "Weed Ma."

"I don't want to read," she said, harsh and breathless as if she'd walked for miles. That was when she saw the shine gathering on the lower lids of his eyes, like rainwater spilling over, and she knew she wasn't the only one who was tired, who wanted to stop running. "How about we get changed," she said in a quieter, even voice. "And I'll tell you a story instead?" She eased him into a lying position, got the package of diapers from her backpack. "A special story with lots and lots of blue things in it?"

"*Bwu,*" said Christopher, somewhat mollified.

"Uh-huh. Blue water and blue starfish and a great big blue octopus."

"*Bwu.*" Christopher picked up the skirt of Flopsy Jo's jumper, studying it where he lay, looking, she realized, for the blue square she'd shown him that morning. She changed his diaper, again wrestling with the tapes that seemed to have been put in the wrong places, then pulled his rabbit from the pack and scooped him into her lap.

"Now, this octopus," she went on, snuggling down with him and Lady Macbeth along the length of the booth, "was friends with a beautiful mermaid. Who, by the way," she added, "had a splendid blue tail.

"Each morning, the two of them would go jogging along the ocean floor. The mermaid wore a Nike sweatshirt, and the octopus had sneakers on all nine of his feet."

"*Bwu?*" inquired Christopher. He ignored the rabbit, found his thumb instead, something she hadn't seen him do before. At the same time, he reached for a strand of her hair, using it like the soft ribbon edge of a blanket, rubbing it against his nose, staring at her through his half-closed eyes.

"Of course," Feena told him. "Blue sneakers with blue laces and blue bells that rang whenever the octopus jogged." He continued staring, though he lost focus, lids drooping until his eyes were nothing but moist slivers of azure. "They ran for miles, those two, over mountains of sand and squashy fields of seaweed."

Lying beside him, Feena knew she couldn't give him up, couldn't risk taking him to the police. What if they didn't believe her? She listened to his even breathing and felt an old tenderness, a secret, buried joy. She remembered that other baby, remembered dropping into his crib, batting his mobile and setting the puffy clowns spinning, whirling above their heads. As her own eyes closed, she remembered, too, throaty baby laughs, like singing bubbles, like the language of birds you could almost understand.

The voice was soft and moany, but Feena couldn't make out the words. Shaking off sleep, she heard it even after she'd opened her eyes. There was someone singing, someone coming toward them, getting closer and closer. By the time she'd sat up, put a finger over Christy's mouth, it was too late. They were face-to-face.

Raylene Watson was alone, unusual enough in itself. But she was singing, too. An almost sweet song that came to a sudden end when she saw Feena and the baby. She threw her head back, then grew visibly stiffer, taller. She hid something she'd been carrying behind her back, and without disguising her disappointment, fixed Feena with her cinnamon stare. "What?" she asked. "You decide to ditch school and home both?"

Christy wriggled down from the booth, and Lady Macbeth tumbled to the ground. He didn't stop to pick her up, but rushed, like the worst kind of traitor, straight to Raylene. Feena was suddenly aware of shame, physical and heavy, swamping her. She was ashamed her lips were chapped, while Raylene's shone like mother-ofpearl. Ashamed the baby's ponytails were again hope-lessly cockeyed, one nearly slipped from its band. "No," she began to ad-lib. "No, I didn't ditch anything." Ashamed that she'd been asleep, that she felt tears still in her eyes, she said, "I just need to watch my...little sister, that's all."

"Here?" Raylene didn't take her hands from behind her back, merely scanned the dusty ruin with her eyes. "If you're waiting for your order, you got a long wait." Her tone was back to the cool crustiness she used in the halls at school. "Cutler's Family Style's been closed five years."

Christy held his arms out, begging to be picked up, and Raylene had a choice to make. Slowly, she bent down, laid a paperback book on the ground beside her, then folded her arms around him. "Hi, Toffee," she said, her voice soft again. "How's my bit of sugar?"

"It's Christy," Feena told her, reaching out, straight-ening the droopiest ponytail. "Her name's Christy."

"Christy." Raylene said it over slowly, as if she were feeling the shape of it in her mouth. "Christy," she asked him then, "you mind if I call you Toffee?"

Feena, who had learned her lesson, glanced only briefly at the book Raylene left behind on the ground. She lifted her backpack off the other side of the booth, making room for the two of them across from her. "Your mom sick?" Raylene asked, deposit-ing Christopher, then walking to the old oven and opening its lopsided door. As if she owned the place, she reached in and took out a can of orange soda, the same brand Feena had seen on the table. "She can't take care of Toffee herself?"

Feena nodded, grabbing the lie Raylene offered. "Just a cold," she said. "But she doesn't want the baby to get it."

"Uh-huh." Raylene took a long sip, lowering the can when Christy begged for some, too. "You plan on spending the night here, or what?"

Raylene listened, with only a hint of a smile, while Feena concocted a story about her mother being too sick to watch the baby but not too sick to be left alone. About how she was sure things would be better by tonight and so they'd go home any minute. It didn't make much sense, but it didn't need to, because why should Raylene care, anyway? Why should she be hanging around them the way she was?

Why, Feena wondered as the sun's buttery haze turned pink and long fingers of shadow spread across the grass, didn't Miss High and Mighty just go away and leave them alone?

But she didn't. She chattered and fussed and played with Christy. She told him about the people who worked at CVS. About the crazy customers, like the woman who came in every day to buy a small jar of baby food for her toothless tabby. When Raylene had asked her why she didn't get seven or eight jars at once, the woman told her she couldn't be sure what kind of food her cat would feel like the next day.

"Would you believe it, Toffee?" Raylene tickled Christopher, rolling him over on the bench. "If I had myself a talking cat like that, it better make up its fuzzy mind, and fast. Not be giving me orders up and down, right?" Then she tickled some more, until the baby giggled, helpless and thrilled, pedaling the air like a racer.

Feena was, she had to acknowledge it, more than a little jealous. Of how Raylene and Christy played, as if they'd known each other forever. Of how the baby followed Raylene's every move, seemed to watch her with the same intensity, the same awe Feena had thought he reserved just for her.

As the minutes passed, she was not only jealous, she was worried. The sun had sunk behind the woods, and her mother, long home, would be wondering about the second note, about her daughter's sudden spurt of popularity.

Part of Feena—the part that read romantic novels and loved adventure—watched her dilemma from above, saw herself as a tragic heroine with a secret no one could share. But another part—the part of her that remembered Lenore's face, the sudden brightness when she'd offered Feena the Chinese food last night— wished she could just go home and go to bed.

"Raylene?" She turned to the other girl now, using the same words, the same voice she had yesterday—had it only been one day?—on the playground with Dale. "Do you think you could do me a favor?"

Raylene looked at her, expressionless again. She seemed to save that vacant stare just for Feena. But Feena was too tired to care. "Do you think you could watch my sister while I run home and check on my mom?"

"You live close?"

Careful. "Close enough."

"Okay, I guess so." Raylene appeared to have a moment's doubt. She checked Christy, who, unfazed by Feena's standing and gathering up her backpack, remained bent over his new books, piling and unpiling them according to some secret baby formula. "But I got a life, you know. Make it quick."

"Sure." Feena shrugged into her backpack, dashed toward the highway. She'd stepped over Raylene's abandoned book and the pieces of broken sign before she turned and went back. She stroked Christy's hair, kissed his forehead. "I'll see you in a little while," she promised. "Thanks, Raylene."

"Yeah. No problem." Feena had cleared the sign again before Raylene yelled after her, "Just get your butt back. Hear?"

nine

.

.

.

.

The sharp smell hit Feena as soon as she walked inside. The bathroom door was open, and her mother stood in front of the mirror over the sink. Wielding a dryer, her mouth pursed, Lenore studied herself, turning slightly as strands of brown hair blew out from her head at crazy angles. She clearly hadn't heard Feena come in.

Feena glanced over her shoulder into the darkened living room. The Sony was on, its colorful glass eye winking away, unwatched. This, in itself, was extraordinary, but what Feena saw when she turned back to the bathroom was horrifying. Spreading from the part in her mother's hair, like an alien mutation spawned in the dryer's heat, was a broad grape-colored stripe. Feena noticed the forest of plastic bottles on the top of the toilet, the box with a photo of a laughing woman whose hair was so bouncy it obviously lit up her life. "Mom?" She said it louder the second time: "Mom!"

The guilty surprise, the trapped expression on her mother's face when she looked up, made Feena want to turn away. Made her wish she could forget this moment forever, so they could go back to normal. When Lenore finally turned off the dryer, they stared at each other, wordless.

Feena recovered first. "Is this a cry for help?" she asked, nodding toward the box of hair coloring. Her voice sarcastic, her arms folded, she felt the panicky thrill of changing roles, of becoming Lenore's exasperated parent.

The broad smile that took the place of that other look, that trapped look, was phony through and through. "Oh, hi, Feen." Lenore, avoiding Feena's eyes, turned back to the mirror, talked to her daughter's reflection instead of the real girl behind her. "I...well, I just thought I'd try a new me. Got tired of the old one." Another forced grin, her eyes sliding from Feena's mirror twin to her own. "What do you think?"

"What do I think?" *What was next? Was her mother going to get a belly ring? A barbed-wire tattoo, like the one on the arm of the boy who sat in front of Feena in geometry?*

"I think you're going to get quite a reaction at the DMV tomorrow."

"Yeah?"

"Yeah." Feena remembered her mother complaining about what "stuffed shirts" the people in her office were. She couldn't imagine what they'd think of Lenore's fluorescent henna job.

"Maybe they need a little shaking up, huh?" Her mother wasn't smiling now, or sheepish, just hopeful.

So hopeful that, even though she wasn't at all sure why, it made Feena want to cry. "Maybe," she agreed, too late.

"Eaten yet?" Lenore brushed past her, headed for the coat closet jammed into the narrow space between the bathroom and the front door. "We could go out." She started rummaging through the sweaters and coats that dangled above an unorganized heap of sneakers, boots, tennis rackets, and a carton of ancient Christmas decorations.

"I can't." Feena hadn't meant it to sound so sharp, so hard. "I've got to get back to my friend's house," she said more gently now. "But I could bring some takeout home with me later if you want."

Her mother backed out of the closet. "No," she said, passing Feena again, finding the couch and the remote. "I guess not." She bent over the control, her bright new hair falling across her face. "Don't bother."

But now, suddenly, Feena wanted to bother. "It wouldn't be any trouble," she said. "Really."

The Sony blinked, and its screen filled with a bowl of pasta and a bottle of spaghetti sauce. Feena stood, caught for a second, as the sauce serenaded the pasta with a booming operatic aria and the spaghetti answered it in a trilling soprano. She tried to come up with something else to say, but all she could think about was Christy and Raylene, waiting. She was nearly to the door when Lenore, without turning around, said, almost to herself, "Nothing's changed at all."

"Huh?" Feena thought maybe her mother was talking to the television.

"Not a goddamn thing is any different," Lenore repeated, still facing the screen. "We pack up our worldly goods, drive a lousy twelve hundred miles, and life still sucks."

"What do you mean?" Feena walked back toward the couch, but not all the way. "Everything's different. We've got a new house. You've got a new job." She took another step forward. "I've got a new school."

Her mother pressed the remote, and the spaghetti and sauce disappeared, replaced by nature footage of a huge bird, its wings spread wide, chasing another bird off the screen. "For two years," an announcer's voice said, "this albatross has defended its decoy love against all comers. Convinced the plastic replica is its mate, the befuddled bird has remained loyal for—" The remote clicked again, and a gospel group was belting out a chorus, "Never again, never again, my Lord. No, never again. Never..."

"Yeah," Lenore said, hardly audible over the music. "I guess things are better for you." She turned to Feena, still clutching the remote. "Are they, Feen? Are they better for you?"

Better! Was changing everything, shuffling it up, and letting it fall anywhere, like a deck of cards, her mother's idea of making life better? For a nanosecond, Feena considered sitting on the couch beside Lenore, telling her in no uncertain terms just how *un*better things were. "Uh-huh." She nodded, thinking of Raylene, picturing the hint of a frown that meant Her Highness was not pleased. "Things are fine, Mom."

Lenore waited, wearing that eager, pork-with-pineapple expression of hers. She wanted more, Feena knew. She needed to hear how leaving the apartment in Connecticut—saying goodbye to Feena's only serious friend, making it nearly impossible for her father to find them if he ever decided to, driving away from the small grave, where no one cut the grass—how all this was a great move. It was as if she had taken everything away so they had nothing left to lose. As if she actually thought it was all for the best.

"I really have to go, Mom." Feena walked again to the door, spoke without looking back. "We'll talk later, okay?" But when she'd shut the door and was running back toward the restaurant, she could still see that silly expectancy, that dumb hope on her mother's face.

Raylene and the baby didn't seem to have missed her at all. They were sitting on a blanket beside a patch of spindly legged echinacea that shot up through the weeds and dense matted grass. Lady Macbeth lay on her side behind them, one bright eye catching the last of the twilight. Both their heads were bent over Raylene's paperback; even Christopher didn't look up until Feena's sneaks stopped at the edge of the blanket. *Where on earth had Raylene gotten a blanket, anyway?*

"And that," Raylene told Christopher, not even glancing at Feena, "is the end of the story." She closed the book and put it to one side. Feena tried to read the title, but all she could see in the quick casual glance she gave it was the picture on the cover. The silhouette of a house on fire. Was it Thornfield Hall?

If Raylene hadn't been Raylene, and if Feena hadn't been trapped in her own awkward self, Feena would have sat down beside them. She would have picked up the book, like any ordinary girl talking to another ordinary girl. "So," she would have said— scrutinizing the cover, checking it out—"what are you guys reading?"

But she didn't. She remained standing at the fringed edge of the blanket, perspiration inching down from her hairline to her ears. "Thanks," she told Raylene, who finally looked up at her. "Thanks a lot for watching my sister."

If it was possible, Raylene seemed more disinterested than ever. "Yeah," she said, standing up too, lifting Christy off the blanket. A smile, forced and unfriendly, as she folded it into methodical, crisp squares. "How's your mother?"

"She's feeling better." Feena bent down as Christy walked over, dragging Lady Macbeth by her felt-lined ears. "Hi, you," she said. "What have you been doing?"

"Weed," Christy told her, picking up the paperback. "Weed book."

"That's good." Feena glanced at the cover again. It was, indeed, the still unreturned "library book." It was *Jane Eyre*. She almost smiled at Raylene, then stopped herself. "Kind of rough reading for a little kid, isn't it?" she asked.

"I left out a lot."

"Hey," Feena told her, remembering the book in her backpack. "Maybe you should try this next." She walked back to the bench, opened the pack, and pulled out the book. "If Christy likes love stories, this is supposed to be great."

For the first time, Feena saw Raylene completely astonished. It was just a second, then there was no surprise, only suspicion. "Where'd you get that book?"

"You dropped it the other day."

"How about that?" Raylene shook her head, waved the book away. "An equal-opportunity reader." She stood, hugging the folded blanket to her chest, a sort of challenge in her level gaze. "Is that supposed to get you a medal?"

"A medal?" What was wrong? What was always so wrong? Why couldn't Feena say or do one thing right?

"Look," Raylene said, "I know you might choke on it, but how about the truth?"

"The truth?" Feena was in echo mode again. Her brain racing, she watched Christy, who was pulling on the edge of the blanket.

"Yeah, you know." Raylene's voice was low and smooth, frightening in its neutrality. "The truth as in: If this is your sister, what are you doing hiding out in a fast-food joint for ghosts?"

"Weed," the baby commanded, but neither of them was listening. "Weed mu."

"I'm not—"

"The truth, as in: How come you turn six shades of pale every time I ask about your mom?"

"Okay. Okay." Feena was cornered, desperate. In seconds, she ran through scores of lies, rejected each one. "What if I told you," she asked at last, "that Christy isn't my sister?"

"I'd say that's a start." Raylene turned, put the folded blanket into a cabinet that lay on its back behind the booth.

"What if I told you she's *my* baby?" Now that she'd said it out loud like that, Feena felt braver, surer. For a while, anyway, it was true. "I'm her mother."

"Yours, huh?" Raylene gave a long, low whistle, then crossed her arms. "Who's the daddy?"

"His name is Edward." Before she could stop herself, Feena was off on a romantic tangent. "He's blind. It was an accident. There was a fire—"

"I read the book." Raylene unfolded her arms, stood impassive. "I swear, either you're a plain fool or you take me for one." She put an arm around Christy, who had crawled up onto the closed cabinet and was kicking its side with his sneaks.

"No, really . . ."

Carefully, painstakingly, Raylene straightened the collar on the baby's dress. "'No, really' nothing," she said. "Your time's up, Miss Books for Brains."

"*Bwu,*" Chris interrupted, pointing to his sneaks. He looked at Raylene for approval. "Cwiss shoes *bwu.*"

Raylene didn't answer, just lifted him off the cabinet and set him on the ground. He tried for Feena's attention now. "*Bwu,*" he said, tugging on the hem of her tee. "Cwiss shoes *bwu.*"

Raylene's gaze was level, menacing. "This baby walked right out of his diapers while you were gone." She paused and there was that nonsmile again. "Course, that's no surprise, seeing how you bought extra large."

That explained the way Raylene was acting. Feena couldn't face her. *The cold voice, the dirty looks.* She glanced away, toward the woods, the dark silhouettes of the trees. "I didn't know diapers came in different sizes," she said softly.

"Buying diapers twice as big as you need is one thing." Raylene spoke slowly, deliberately. "But nobody's too dumb to know a girl from a boy."

"It's not what you think..." Feena felt Christy's eagerness, his impatient yanking on her shirt. But she couldn't look down at him, couldn't take her tear-filled gaze off the woods.

"I figure you got that stuff pretty well sorted out before you went and made this baby in the first place." Raylene never took her dark, mirror eyes off Feena. "I figure you can't be one-half as dumb as you act."

"I'm not." Feena heard the frogs start up, was aware of a moth tumbling, mud-colored, in the dusk beside her. "I mean, you see, it's just—"

"And I figure maybe you need some serious help. But one thing there's no maybe about. One thing I know as sure as I know my name. You won't be taking this child anywhere, anymore." Finally, turning from Feena, Raylene leaned down, took Christy's hand, and drew him into her arms.

"But I..." *She knows,* Feena thought numbly. *She'll call the police and that will be the end.*

"I've seen some sick, sorrowful rejects, but I never seen anyone lower than you." Christopher wriggled in Raylene's fierce grasp, but she held him tight, pinning him against her.

"You don't understand." *They'll take him away, and then they'll arrest me.* Feena considered grabbing the baby back, pictured the two of them running off, streaking into the night. But her legs felt weak, too wobbly to carry one person, much less two. *They'll arrest me,* she told herself, *and he'll have to go back.*

"Anyone burns a baby like that don't deserve spit."

"Burns?" The numb place in Feena dissolved, and suddenly there was room for Raylene's anger. She saw it in the other girl's face, felt it in her own chest. "What do you mean, 'burns'? What are you talking about?"

"That moron act of yours just won't wash." Feena moved toward them, but Raylene pulled the baby back and stood in front, protecting him. "Next, you're gonna tell me those cigarette burns on Toffee's legs happened by themselves, right? Just a bad case of diaper rash, right?"

Feena stopped, stood still. "Oh, my god!" She looked at Christy, who was now holding his hands out to Feena, trying to get free of Raylene's grasp. She remembered the red weepy constellation on his thigh. How could she have been so stupid?

And how, she asked herself, could anyone in the whole, bewildering world be so cruel? She shut her eyes, grew dizzy fighting the pictures—images of Christy held fast in his mother's immense arms, of her glowing cigarette tip moving up and down, up and down. "That'll teach you, Mister. That'll teach you to do what I say."

ten

.

.

.

No go." Christy was repeating it over and over now. "Cwiss no go." He wasn't yelling; he never yelled. But he was pulling away from Raylene, setting all his weight against her. "Want stay," he insisted, tugging, looking over his shoulder toward Feena. Finally, Raylene gave up trying to drag him. She secured her book under one arm, then stooped down and grabbed him around the waist, hoisted him up still kicking like a struggling pig. They had set off into the gloom before Feena realized what had happened.

"Wait!" Feena gathered up the books and stumbled after them. "Give me a chance!" She tripped over the pieces of sign she'd forgotten about, was caught by a thorny creeper that bordered the path to the highway. "Give me a chance! I can explain!"

If she heard her, Raylene gave no indication. In fact, she picked up speed, and Feena was afraid she'd lose them. It was hard to run and yell at the same time, but she couldn't let them disappear. It was so dark now that she was glad Christy kept up his protests. "No!" she heard him scolding. "Want here, Ween. Want here!"

"Raylene, please!" She followed behind as the older girl struck off down the path, away from the road. "He needs me! You've got to stop!"

When Raylene turned around and started walking back toward her, Feena gasped with relief. She stood, head bent, as Raylene—calm, unflappable Raylene—screamed.

"No, *you* got to stop. You got to stop lying. You got to stop chasing after us. And most of all, you got to stop treating this baby like dirt."

Feena didn't care. She let the tears come, let them run down her face. "I didn't. I didn't," she said in between sobs. "I was trying to stop it. I took him away." She buried her face in her hands, smelling the sharp, dark sap of the creepers she'd uprooted as she raced after them.

"What trash are you talking now?" Raylene stood close. She put Christy down but held tight to his hand.

"I didn't hurt him," Feena said, lowering her hands, trying to see Raylene's face by the new moon. "I would never hurt him." She hardly noticed Christy edging toward her, didn't know he was there until his small pincer fingers found her shirt. Gratefully, she lifted him up, held him tight, cried into his baby neck. "You have to listen to me, please."

Raylene, still holding Christy by one arm, waited. "Well?" she said.

Feena blinked into the dark, still fighting tears. She talked rapidly, tripping over her words, afraid she might lose her audience. But Raylene didn't move, just stood and listened.

Feena told it all, without editing, without trying to explain or excuse what she'd done. To name it, to say it out loud was enough. It was as if Raylene were a quiet, empty vessel into which Feena could pour it all—the fear, the mistakes, the second thoughts. Bit by bit, drop by drop, she told her everything—the move from Connecticut, the humiliation of the Pizza Hut, the short-tempered woman, and the little boy with her dead brother's name.

As Feena talked, Raylene let go Christy's hand, let him relax into her. Behind the whispery safety of his curls, Feena kept going, as if the story had been waiting to burst free. She described the night in the miniature-golf booth, the trips for food and supplies, the newspapers that hadn't mentioned a missing child.

By the time she reached their morning in the library, she'd stopped crying, started wishing she had a tissue to wipe away the mess streaming from her nose. "We even got a library card," she told Raylene, letting Christy down to retrieve something shiny he'd seen on the ground. "Pretty funny," she added, rubbing a hand across her face, "how guilty I felt giving a false name." She glanced nervously at her listener. "I mean, considering everything else I've done."

Feena waited then, finally out of words. Raylene waited, too. Was she calculating, judging?

Only Christopher moved, busy with the piece of coconut husk he'd found. Slipping into sandbox mode, he used the shell to dig in the dirt, undaunted by the slow progress he was making with the hard, baked earth. "Make mu," he chanted, patting the small mound he'd managed to pile up. "Cwiss make mu and mu and mu."

"Well," Raylene announced with the same economy, the same slow, sure drawl she always used, "it wasn't in the paper on account of nobody reported it."

"What do you mean?"

"Whoever burned Toffee has been turned into DYFS a zillion times. They know the cops won't believe them."

"Difuss?" asked Feena. "What's Difuss?"

"Division of Youth and Family Services." Raylene looked down at Christy, kicked a tuft of dried grass with one sandaled foot. "You know, caseworkers, checker-uppers, all that. Toffee's mom probably figured out she'll be Suspect Number One the minute she goes to the police."

Of course! Feena had never even considered that, but it made sense. If the sweet-faced woman had been reported for child abuse, she might not have told anyone her son was missing. And the police wouldn't be looking for Christy, after all!

"Toffee, let me see your sugar face." Raylene stooped down and cupped Christy's chin, distracting him from his earth moving. "Lord, I wonder can I ever get used to you being a boy." She sounded as though someone had switched the ending of a fairy tale on her. She sighed, then looked up at Feena. "It's not right, is it?" she asked in a soft voice Feena hardly recognized. "Some folks would do anything to have a baby, but they can't. And some that have kids, well..." She trailed off. "They shouldn't, that's all."

Feena nodded. The mosquitoes were like night armies now, attacking from all sides. Just off the path, in the woods, something rustled through the grass.

"When my mother got pregnant?" Raylene took off her smock, folded it under her, and sat down, waiting for Christy to finish playing. "I mean, the second time? She spent three months in bed. She said she almost lost me and she wasn't about to take a chance like that again. Three months lying there, 24/7." She laughed gently. "Going crazy and making me that way, too."

"How old were you?" Feena sat down near her, not even bothering about the dirt. She wrapped her arms around her knees.

"Ten." Raylene patted the side of Christy's mud mound. "That's good, Toffee. That's real good."

"So?"

"So what?"

"So did you get a brother, or a sister?"

"Didn't get either one." Raylene's voice dropped lower still. "Mama had a miscarriage."

Feena heard the intake of her own breath. "I'm sorry."

"We had this room all painted, you know?" Raylene wasn't looking at Christy or even at Feena now. She was talking to herself, her eyes liquid in the moonlight. "My mother, she wanted everything lemon yellow, so it wouldn't matter, boy or girl. But I just knew it was going to be a girl. I saved up and got this lamp made out of a glamour doll. She had a yellow dress with white lace, and Mama let me put it on the baby's dresser."

"Oh, god." Real life, Feena was learning faster than she wanted, is full of sad things—sad small things that people never read about, or see on TV.

"There was so much blood the day it happened." Raylene stopped, watching Christy busily work beside her. "Mama was crying and groaning and asking me to help. I couldn't do anything." Another pause, Christy pounding away at the mud. "In the end, all I could do was call the ambulance."

"Where was your dad?" Feena thought of her own father, his bedtime story, the one he hadn't read but recited slow and quiet as a prayer. *Once upon a time there was a baby. One day, he had to leave his family . . .*

"My dad?" Raylene's voice got harder fast, took on an edge. "You mean Mister Postcard? Who knows?" She sighed and looked, finally, straight at Feena. "He moved in and out of our lives so much, I changed shoe sizes between visits. I don't think he even knew Mama was pregnant.

"And guess what?" A half laugh caught low in her throat. "Turns out, it wasn't just one. The doctor said it was twins. Girls, twin girls. Isn't that something? We only picked out one name, Mama and me. And all along, I had two baby sisters waiting to get born."

"Raylene . . ." Feena wanted to hug her. To pull her close like she did Christy and hold her tight. "I'm so sorry."

"Bad part was, Mama couldn't talk about it after. She didn't even want to name the other baby. I begged and begged, but she told me it didn't matter, anyhow.

"I named her, though." The softer, younger voice had crept back; Feena leaned in to hear. "And then I wrote a letter to each of those babies. On account of I wanted to say goodbye."

"Bye." Christy left his digging to scrooch closer to Raylene. "Bye, Ween," he told her, waving cheerfully.

"I made a funeral." Raylene put her arm around the baby, handed him the coconut piece he'd dropped. "I buried that glamour-doll lamp along with the letters. Dug a hole in the woods, back behind our house." Christy had begun a new project now, digging in the triangle of ground between his legs. Raylene took her arm from around him, wiped at her eyes. "I guess it was pretty dumb. I mean, there was no coffin and no bodies. And that hole I dug? It was so small, I had to take the shade off to fit the lamp in.

"I didn't care, though." She kept brushing at her eyes—first one, then the other. "I wanted my sisters to have names. Names and something pretty all their own."

Maybe it was the tears. Or the way Raylene looked down now, away from Feena. But suddenly it was easy. To reach out without thinking. To put her arms around her, to rock her like an infant. "Oh, Ray." Feena was startled by the way the nickname spilled out. "Ray."

For a second, a shiver of sweetness, they stayed like that. Feena inhaled a light rosy scent that could have been perfume or just Raylene. And for an instant, the other girl's whole body relaxed, as if she were going to fall asleep in Feena's arms.

Then it was over. Christy was tugging on Feena's sleeve and Raylene was on her feet, dusting off her skirt. "Come on," she said briskly. "We got to get going." She tied her smock around her waist, picked up her book, and began walking in the same direction she'd been headed before.

"Where?" Feena got to her feet, too, then picked up Christy. There was a lot she wanted to ask. Had Raylene's mother had other children? Where was Raylene's dad now? But there was no time. All she could do was dash after the flapping red smock ahead of her, hoping to keep up with it in the dark.

They followed the little trail that twisted around palms and large, spiked clusters of pampas grass. Feena's ankles were itching and probably bleeding. But she kept lunging ahead, afraid she'd lose her way completely if Raylene got too far ahead.

"Toffee needs something to eat, a place to sleep. And we got to figure a way to take care of her...him during the day."

"We"? What had Feena missed? When had Christy become a group project? "Wait a minute. I have to—"

"Hurry up, can't you?" Raylene was charging, sure-footed, along the path as if she knew every inch of it. "Maybe *you* can stay out all night, but my mother's radar kicks in and the sirens start blasting at nine o'clock. Sharp." She turned and stopped in front of a smaller path, a muddy little hint of a trail.

"What?" Feena was glad to slow down, to adjust the backpack that had been slamming against her right shoulder blade. She couldn't see the moon now, had no idea where they were.

"My mother," Raylene explained. "She does this terminator thing if I'm not home on time. First, she worries. Then she goes ballistic."

Mother! Feena had forgotten all about Lenore. Had she fallen asleep in front of the TV? What if Feena wasn't there when she woke up?

Raylene turned, pointed to a dim light up ahead. "There," she said, as if she'd read Feena's mind. "Call home."

"Home?" Feena shifted Christy's weight against her hip, following Raylene toward the fuzzy light until it became a phone booth beside a small parking lot, the asphalt sparkling and shining like a pond all around them.

"Yeah. You're spending the night with me."

"I am?"

"No, course not. But that's what you tell your mother, see?"

"I can't." Christy was heavier than Feena could remember him being. She unloaded him, standing him on his feet beside her. "She won't believe me."

Christy held up his hands, not to be picked up again, but to twirl, like a dizzy top, around and around the lot. Free of tangles and creepers, reveling in the sudden light, he spun drunkenly from Feena to Raylene and back again.

"What do you mean, she won't believe you?" Raylene sighed, arms folded in that familiar warrior stance of hers.

Feena waited for the right words, watching Christy and then the small, fierce cloud of insects that circled the light above them. "She won't believe me because I never have friends over," she explained. "And no one here has ever asked me to spend the night."

Another sigh. Different, gentler. Raylene let Christy run at full tilt into her arms. "Well, now they have," she said.

eleven

.

.

.

Lenore sounded hoarse, foggy with sleep when she answered the phone. Feena had to say it twice, "I'm going to spend the night at a friend's, Mom." *No fancy add-ons. You don't get caught if you keep it simple.*

Feena could hear the baby and Raylene behind her. "Want mik," Christy was saying. "Want mik, peese." *Milk* was the word he used for anything to eat and drink. It had been hours, Feena realized, since they'd done either.

"What do you mean? What friend?"

"She, uh, goes to my school." *Simple isn't the same as stupid, stupid.* "She's a sophomore." *Older is good. Older is more responsible.*

"Today was laundry day." Lenore sounded whiny, disappointed. "I saved your stuff. I'm not doing your dirty clothes, Feen."

Raylene was walking the baby farther and farther away as his protests got louder. But Feena could still hear him. Not crying so much as indignant. "Mik, more mik!"

"No. Sure, Mom," Feena said into the receiver. "I'll do the laundry. Don't worry."

"You better. And Feen?"

Feena waited. What if Lenore asked for her friend's name? What if she wanted a phone number?

"Have a good time, okay?"

Feena hung up, relieved and guilty. As she followed Raylene and Christy back into the woods, as the light from the phone booth grew pale behind them, she wondered whether there was enough leftover Chinese. She knew how tired her mother got after work, how she hated going out again.

"This is it." Raylene pulled up short in front of her, pointing through the brush. They walked toward the gleam of water, and there, mired in a shallow stream, was the most dilapidated boat Feena had ever seen.

It looked like a shrimp boat, though how a shrimp boat had ended up in a marshy Florida swamp, she could never have explained. When they cleared the woods completely and the moon shone on the old hull, stranded like a beached fish half in and half out of the water, all Feena knew was that it was perfect.

"I come here sometimes," Raylene told her while Feena and Christy studied the rotting deck, the tiny cabin clinging to one end as if it might slip any minute into the sludge.

"Boat," Christy announced a bit uncertainly, leaning toward the apparition.

"Yes," Feena agreed. "A bed boat. Let's go see."

The planks on what was left of the deck swayed like a tree house in the wind when they stepped on board. Across the narrow strip of swamp, some night bird whooped with a deep, doglike cry. Raylene led the way to the cabin, pushed open one of its shuttered doors. Feena noticed a weather-beaten sign on the other. CAPTAIN'S QUARTERS, it said in letters the weak moon turned the blue of a well-loved baby blanket. NO LANDLUBBERS ALLOWED. Had this wreck, she wondered, once been someone's idea of a pleasure boat?

Inside, though, was a different story. Raylene had outfitted her reading nook with pillows and a quilt on the built-in bunk. Under the porthole window were a pile of paperbacks and a glass oil lamp. In shelves along the wall behind the dining bench were water and juice bottles, a portable radio, and boxes of cookies and crackers. The place was clean, cozy, and the most romantic hideout imaginable. Even the musky smell from the marsh and the boat's mildewed wood seemed exotic.

"Oh," Feena said, stepping to the center of the small room and whirling in happy circles like a dervish. "Oh, my gosh."

"You should be safe here," Raylene told her. "Nobody knows about this place." She hoisted Christy toward the low ceiling so he could touch the ancient lantern that swung from its center. Someone had placed a fat candle there, and someone had burned it countless times. Great folds of green wax had melted around its edges and dripped through the grill.

After she'd put the baby on the bed, Raylene took a pack of matches from the table and lit the candle. A delicious amber light bounced into the corners of the room and along the dark timbers of the ceiling. "I got to go," she said. "I'll be back in the morning, though, in time for you to get to school."

"School?" The halls of Washanee seemed a thousand miles away. At the thought of going back there, Feena blinked, like some cave bat used to the dark.

"Course. You keep cutting, they're bound to figure something's up. They'll send someone to your house."

"What about you?" Feena asked.

"I'm okay. Besides, we'll take turns. One day on; one day off. Got it?"

"Got it."

But Feena didn't really get it. Not right away. Even

after Raylene had rubbed Vaseline on Christy's burns, then changed him; even after she'd showed them where she kept cups and plastic forks and knives; even after she'd kissed the baby, waved goodbye, and was long gone, down some trail Feena could only guess at, it hardly seemed real.

Safe. Could it really happen? If she didn't think about tomorrow, if she let herself relax into Raylene's take-charge confidence, Feena felt it could. Once she and Christy had eaten, Feena snuggled next to him under the quilt in the sea bunk, whispering like a counselor to a brand-new camper after lights out. "Isn't this great, Chris? Won't we have fun here?"

It took two stories this time—one about Lady Macbeth and one about a band of gypsy moths (Feena was inspired by the fuzzy dive-bombers that kept throwing themselves against the lantern)—before Christy's eyes shut and his breathing deepened beside her.

It took much longer, though, for Feena to fall asleep. Exhausted as she was, she lay wakeful and dizzy with gratitude, feeling the warmth of Christy's body curled next to hers, staring at the shadows that splashed across the ceiling as the boat rocked in the wind. She thought about Raylene, pictured her tucked away here afternoons, singing in that sweet moany voice she'd overheard. She imagined her reading, devouring romantic moments just the way Feena herself did when she hid out with her books.

And then she remembered the twins. She could still see Raylene's dark head buried in Christopher's curls. "Some folks would do anything to have a baby."

The stranded boat bobbed underneath her. Fingers of wind poked in through the timbers and stroked her forehead. And still she couldn't sleep. Stealthily, deftly, Feena slipped out from under the comforter and dug in her pack. She pulled out Raylene's book and, sitting at the table under the lamp, began it once more:

So Janie waited a bloom time, and a green time and an orange time. But when the pollen again gilded the sun and sifted down on the world she began to stand around the gate and expect things. . . . She often spoke to falling seeds and said, "Ah hope you fall on soft ground," because she had heard seeds saying that to each other as they passed.

Hours later, when Feena had finished and finally looked up, surfacing slowly from Janie Woods's life, returning to the lapping of the waves and the moist creakiness of the boat, she felt as if she'd brought a little bit of Janie's courage with her. Through hurricanes and rabies, through death and disease, this new heroine had saved a place inside herself, a place the world could never touch.

Finally, after she'd slipped back into bed beside Christy, Feena drifted off. In her dream, she heard deep laughter, saw Janie Woods, her dusky face lovely and proud as Raylene's. Janie stood on the deck of the marooned shrimp boat, which, preposterously, was sailing out from the swamp toward the ocean. Next to her, Feena dreamed a less graceful, a paler figure. Hidden by a flapping bonnet and a gray dress that swelled like a bell to her feet, Jane Eyre took Janie's hand, and together they turned toward the sky, swollen with clouds as black as bruises. Undaunted, the two of them watched the lightning blanch the night, and fearless, they threw back their heads and laughed for pure joy as the boat pulled away from shore.

"You glued to this bed?"

Feena opened her eyes. The face looking down on them was not laughing. "If you don't shake your sorry booty," Raylene told her, "a truant officer's going to be knocking on your mom's door before you're in your shoes." She held out her arms to Christopher, who, yawning, held his out, too, and was lifted out of bed.

"What time is it?" Feena realized she'd forgotten to set the radio's alarm. "Am I late?"

Raylene and Christy adjourned to the table. Raylene poured cereal into a bowl. "Not if you hustle," she said, yawning herself. "What you want to do today, Toffee?" she asked the baby, who clearly didn't want to do anything but eat. "Wait up. There's no milk on that yet."

"I don't have any clothes," Feena announced, struggling out of the bunk.

Raylene stared at her. "Looks to me like you're wearing some," she said, turning back to Christy.

"This is the same stuff I wore yesterday," Feena complained. She examined her slept-in shirt, then glanced longingly at Raylene's pink sundress and matching sandals. When her eyes met the other girl's, she turned away, busied herself with the blanket and sheets.

"What?" Raylene asked, not unpleasantly. "You expecting to switch clothes?" She laughed. "You think that shirt would work for me?"

"Huh?" Feena, fumbling for her socks and sneaks, didn't even look up.

"Yeah." Raylene reached across Christopher for the backpack she'd brought, undid the strap. "Just what I need. Some Yankee T-shirt talking Yankee trash. 'Ski Storrs.' What is *that*?"

Feena laughed, looked up. "It's a town in Connecticut. If it doesn't snow, they make it with machines."

Raylene handed Feena a neatly folded skirt and sleeveless shirt. "Here."

"What's this?"

"Go on." She pushed the pile of clothes into Feena's arms. "I figured you didn't bring any."

Thankful, embarrassed, Feena avoided looking at Raylene while she dressed. She managed the zipping and buttoning quickly, anxious to keep her thick waist and pasty flesh under wraps. But Raylene and the baby didn't even notice; they were too absorbed in crackling and popping. Christopher was already on his second bowl of cereal when Feena picked up her own backpack.

"Better take that lunch ticket I left by the door." Raylene still hadn't looked up, was bent over her own bowl. "It's the last day of the week, so you might as well use it. Toffee and me, we're going to find us some real food today."

Feena was astounded and grateful. As usual, Raylene had thought of everything. "That's so nice," she said. "You didn't have to..."

But Raylene put her hand up, looked at her from under thick brows. "You keep talking, you'll be late." She wiped off the baby's milk mustache with a practiced, perfectly timed pass in between spoonfuls. "And if you're late, you have to stay after. I got to be at work at three-thirty. Hear?"

Feena stopped stammering, chastened. "Okay," she said. "I'll come right back." A bit more stammering. A kiss for Christy, and she was gone, blinking in the sun on deck, then setting off down a tiny footpath Raylene promised would bring her to the parking lot behind the grandstand that lined one side of Washanee's soccer field.

twelve

.

.

.

Through the day that followed, Feena was half in, half out—listening as an eager substitute teacher tried desperately to make English matter to a roomful of nail biters, doodlers, and semiprofessional nappers; wondering, at the same time, where Raylene had taken Christopher. Were they at the library, using the new card Feena had left them? Or had Raylene opted for the playground and sandbox?

At lunch, she was grateful all over again for the lunch ticket Raylene had handed her. She was ravenous and completely unfazed by finding no one to sit next to. She took her egg salad sandwich, potato chips, and orange cupcake to one of the weathered benches in a palm-shaded spot just outside the cafeteria's back entrance. Beside the bench was a huge bougainvillea bush, threatening to bring down the trellis to which it clung. Under the long, bloody fingers of blooms was a granite stone with a carved plaque. GRADUATES' GARDEN, CLASS OF '95.

A pair of white butterflies, like willful petals, chased each other across Feena's field of vision. A boy she didn't know, big-boned, with a face the color of boiled ham, came and sat on a bench across from her. They wrinkled their sandwich papers, popped their soda cans, then chewed in silence.

Occasionally, Feena noticed, the boy glanced in her direction, his eyes sliding away from hers if she looked up to catch him. As if the whole thing were an accident and he'd only intended to study the brick wall of the cafeteria or the crusty bark of the palm tree next to her.

It was probably the clothes, Feena reasoned, Raylene's lime and grape skirt, the green shirt that was a little too tight. She shifted on the bench, trying to cover her muddy sneaks with the long, elegant folds of the skirt. How she wished she had the sense, the nerve, to choose colors like that!

She fidgeted and fussed with her sandwich, trying to eat slowly. It was almost a relief when another girl came out of the cafeteria and walked over to the boy. She kissed him on one ham-cheek, sat down beside him, then smiled at Feena.

Feena's minifantasy dissolved, and her whole body relaxed. She was no longer on display, and she dug into her sandwich, taking huge, greedy bites, yielding to the hunger it seemed she'd stored up for days.

In defiance of the happy couple across from her, she finished her first lunch and went back for a second, returning to the bench to chomp fast and furiously and to consider what a rich, confusing mess she'd made of her life.

Why was she sitting here worrying about going to jail instead of what color lip-gloss went with her shoes? And why, in the name of cheerleaders and prom queens everywhere, had she taken it upon herself to right the world's wrongs? Why was she the only girl at Washanee who was praying for school to be over so she could race off and change diapers?

Well, not the only one, she realized. While Feena was eating for both of them at school, Raylene was probably trying to coax Christy out of the sandbox. Or back to the boat. Babysitting and hiding out couldn't be Raylene's top choices for things to do on your day off, but, hard as it was to believe, she was now a bona fide partner in Feena's crime.

"Here you are. I checked every single table inside." Nella Beaufort looked nervously at the golden couple on the other bench, then asked Feena, "Where have you been, anyway?"

Feena was relieved when the lovebirds looked up and noticed she had a friend, even if it was only Nella. Nella, who sat next to Feena three times a week for history, avoided all primary colors in favor of gray shorts and black tees, and was, if possible, even more distracted and lonely than Feena herself.

"I'm on my second sandwich and my third bag of chips." Feena moved over, and Nella slipped onto the bench beside her.

"So?"

"So, I just didn't feel like binging in public, that's all." The solicitous worry on Nella's face somehow annoyed Feena.

"No," Nella explained. "I mean, where were you yesterday? Why weren't you here for the New Deal test?" She peered at Feena from under the layer of thick bangs that nearly hid her eyes. "Were you sick?"

Feena shook her head, popped another chip into her mouth. "Not really," she said. "I had to help my mom with some stuff, that's all." It didn't matter too much what alibi she used, since, like Feena, Nella didn't know many people to pass it on to.

"Yeah," Feena added when Nella continued to look at her expectantly. "She needed a color consultation. She decided to do a punk stripe in her hair."

"Really?" Nella brightened. "How's she look?"

Feena shrugged, and Nella grabbed the chance. "Hey, do you think you could come over after school and help me? I've had this henna kit for three months, but I'm kind of scared to do it.

"You know," she said, when Feena, in turn, sat silent. "A second opinion?"

"I can't."

"You never can." Nella's tiny features pulled tight together. "I guess you like blacks better than your own kind, huh?"

"What?"

"I saw you and that black girl, that Raylene, in the park yesterday."

"So?" *Had she seen Christy, too? Who else had spotted them? Feena could have sworn they'd left the park before school got out. What had gone wrong?*

"Why're you hanging out with her?" Nella seemed genuinely perplexed. "They just want to be white, you know."

" 'They?' "

"Negroes," Nella said, resurrecting a word Feena had only read in books. "Black pride and all that stuff? It's not about that, not really." Nella's tiny pale face had pulled itself into a frown. "What it really is, they all want to be white, like us."

Feena stood up. Did Nella mean what she was saying? Did anyone really believe things like this? "Listen," she said, "I have to go." She balled up her sandwich wrapper and empty chips bag, threw them on her tray.

"Course, they can't be." Nella gathered her own things, stood up, too. "But that don't stop them trying."

Feena wasn't sure whether she wanted to laugh or yell. Mostly, she thought, it wasn't worth doing either one. All she wanted now was to get away, to go back to the boat.

But Nella closed in on her. "You just got to set them straight, is all." She sounded reasonable, patient, someone explaining things to a child. "If you're too nice, they take advantage."

Feena whirled on her ex-friend now, her lunch tray between them like a shield. She'd made her choice, she realized; she'd decided to yell. "Well, of course," she told Nella, her voice rising, the couple across from them untwining themselves to stare. "We better make sure everybody knows where they belong, right?"

Nella looked surprised, thrown off by the question.

"Sure." Feena answered it herself. "Otherwise, someone like Raylene is going to jump at the chance to be like me and you."

"What?" Nella backed away, but Feena spoke louder still.

"It makes perfect sense, doesn't it?" She brushed past Nella, heading for the cafeteria. "Somebody with a killer body, the hottest clothes in school, and tons of friends? It figures she'd probably give just about anything to be"—Feena, laughing at last, shook her head—"like us!"

"Hey." Nella picked up her own tray, followed Feena. "I'm just trying to help, give you the picture, is all."

And suddenly Feena *had* the picture. Raylene walking with a swing, like Janie Woods, straight through all the small people and their small talk. Raylene hiding out, even before Christopher, tucked away in the shells of abandoned restaurants and boats. Like some sort of exotic bird, hiding its plumage, ashamed of its flash. She elbowed the door and rushed inside. She didn't look behind her to see if Nella—small-faced, anxious Nella—was still following. She couldn't have cared less.

Raylene and Christy were bent over a book when Feena got back to the boat. "End the," Raylene read, without looking up. "Mama kissing and hugging, picking banjo, blowing trombone, playing piano..." She was turning the pages of Christopher's favorite book from back to front.

Feena stood, her head cocked, only vaguely recognizing what she heard.

"...dancing, singing a have I." Seeing her now, Christy slammed the book with his hand, beaming. "Weed," he told her. "Ween weed."

"You two are definitely perverted." Feena shook her head, smiling.

Raylene smiled, too. "Look," she explained, "if you'd read this book as many times as I have today, you'd be reading it backwards, too." She closed the book, put it on the table. "How was school?"

"Well, Mommy," Feena told her, "I was a good girl and studied hard."

"Yeah, yeah, yeah," Raylene said. "Any hotties put the moves on you?" She was grinning now, conspiratorial.

"Boys?"

Raylene nodded, waiting.

"Well." Feena, eager to please, remembered the boy outside the cafeteria. "This one guy..."

"Yeah?"

"I think he liked the way I looked." Feena was uncomfortable now, knew she was making a big deal out of nothing. "I guess it was this skirt."

Raylene gave her an appraising look. "Good on you," she said.

"Pretty." Christy ran to her, buried his head in the folds of the skirt. "Feen pretty."

Feena was stunned. It was the first time she'd heard the baby use her name. She looked at Raylene.

"We worked on names today." Raylene picked up a paper plate with the remains of what looked like a Big Mac on it and threw it in a garbage bag by the door. "I figure Toffee's got to know his family now."

"Family?" Feena stared. "Family?"

"Sure." Raylene sat down on the other side of Christy, who had crawled between them. "If he's going to start over, he needs a new family, doesn't he?"

"Start over?" Feena was doing it again. Why was she always reduced to repeating what Raylene said?

"Think about it, Feena." (Another first that Feena registered with only mild surprise. Raylene, too, had never called her by name.) "Why can't Toffee have a say in what happens? I mean, why can't he be the first kid with a vote?"

"You mean"—Feena could hardly say it—"*keep* him?"

Raylene folded her arms and looked levelly at Feena. "If you got a better idea, I'd like to hear it."

"Well, I...We can't. It's against the law."

"Funny, huh?" The tough voice, the hard words were back. "The law don't stop people from burning their kids."

"But—"

"But nothing. I've seen it. My aunt runs a daycare center, and I help her sometimes. I see little girls playing with those pea-size families in the dollhouse. Know how they play?"

Feena didn't answer.

"Last time I was there, this one girl, maybe eight, picks up the mommy doll and talks for her. 'Oh, Lord,' she says, 'Daddy's trying to come back.'

"So the other girl picks up an old lady doll. 'Child,' she says, 'you better get a restraining order.'

"'No,' says the girl with the mother doll, 'that wouldn't do no good. The court would just throw it out.'" Raylene stopped, looked at Feena. "The girl talking for the old lady doll was maybe six."

Feena shook her head. "Six," she repeated. "I was six when my dad left. My mother told me he'd gotten a divorce and wouldn't see us anymore, and I thought he was sick." How little she'd been, how far from understanding. "I thought divorce must be this awful disease and Daddy was going to die."

"I could talk to my aunt." Raylene was pressing her case, closing in. "I'll tell her Toffee is your kid. We can work it out."

Again, Feena shook her head. She looked at Christy, who was rubbing himself against her like a kitten, studying the last page of his piano book. One day, one sweet day was all she'd wanted to give him. Could they really keep him? Could they give him years?

Raylene was looking at Christy too. "You and me, we've seen stuff. We know too much. We watched those towers tumble down like sandcastles on TV. But this child here? He never saw that. He's like a new beginning. A fresh start.

"Think it over, okay?" Raylene stood up and kissed Christy on the top of his head. "I got to go. Just think about it."

And Feena did. Next day and then the whole weekend, while she and Raylene juggled Christopher back and forth, the most cooperative of hostages, she thought of nothing else. At home, wolfing down meals and then racing out again, ignoring the baffled, hurt look on her mother's face, she imagined what it would be like to run away with Christy. On Monday at school, in the last row of every class and alone in the cafeteria, Feena dreamed of watching the baby grow up. On Tuesday, in the boat, like a shady nest, with the baby chattering beside her, she pictured the three of them living a whole new life in a whole new town.

She saw it all in her mind, the years ahead. First, Christy, home from kindergarten, arms filled with drawings of Aunty Raylene and Aunty Feena for the refrigerator (a refrigerator, Feena was determined, that would never be empty). Next, Christy in grade school, filthy from playground triumphs, graduated from sandcastles to kickball. Then finally, in a sort of dim and sentimental fog, she saw Christy in high school, handsome and loving, pursued by girls who all seemed silly and superficial compared with his beloved aunts.

Feena and Raylene checked the papers every day, and every day it seemed more possible, this mythical fresh start. Until Thursday, when Raylene came back from school with the newspaper in her hand. Until she slammed it down on the table, startling Feena and tumbling the precarious "partment" Christy had built with empty milk cartons. "Damn," Raylene told them. "Just plain damn."

"What?" Feena picked up the paper Raylene had folded to the third page. She saw it right away. A small article, tucked into the bottom right-hand corner. MOTHER REPORTS MISSING CHILD.

"Fall down boom," Christy announced, adaptable as ever. "All down boom." He picked up his cartons and began stacking them on top of each other again.

"You said that right, Toffee." Raylene sank onto the bench, picked up one of the small cartons, and studied it, avoiding Feena's worried look. "You sure enough said that right."

thirteen

.

.

.

They didn't learn much from the article. Just the age and the name of the pink-armed woman: *Delores Pierson, 32.* ("Old enough to know better," Raylene said each time they read over the same short paragraph.) And they learned something else, something Feena grabbed at: *of 10 Bide A Bit Village.* "I'm going over there," she announced as soon as she'd spotted the address. "I'm going to go see where Christy lives."

"Are you crazy?" It was not really a question. Raylene stood up, unintentionally toppling the beginnings of a new apartment. "You want to land us both in jail?"

"I won't talk to anyone," Feena promised. "I just want to find out."

"Find out what?"

"I don't know." Feena stared at Christy patiently reassembling his tower. "Where he came from. How bad it is. Stuff like that."

"Why?" The old, stern look was back. "Those burns don't tell you all you need to know?"

Feena felt flushed with doubt, disloyalty. She couldn't stop thinking about the way Christy had looked when they read *Mama's Music*, the way he'd grabbed at his favorite page as if he wanted to pull the round woman right off her piano bench.

"I just want to be sure," she told Raylene. "I want to feel right about what we're doing."

"Well, *time* is what we'll be doing if you go sniffing around out there." Raylene looked at Christy, too. "Do you want what's best for this child?"

Feena nodded.

"What's best is us. You *got* to know that. Don't you?" Raylene pulled her CVS smock out of her book bag and slipped her arms through the sleeves. "I mean, we've got a responsibility here."

Feena nodded, chastened. And then, perhaps because Raylene sounded so much like an adult, or perhaps because she finally noticed the work clothes Raylene was putting on, Feena thought of her mother. Lenore's patience was wearing thin. If Raylene didn't come right back to relieve her, there was no telling what would happen. Especially after yesterday.

Even though Feena had been trying to make the little time she spent with Lenore count, and even though she'd been waking up earlier and earlier so she could sneak out of the house without explanations or arguments, her mother had caught her Wednesday morning.

"Is that you?" It was one of those dumb questions people ask when they're half asleep. "It's still dark outside." Lenore's bathrobe sash had trailed behind her into the kitchen, snakelike. "What are you doing up so early?"

"I...I just wanted to get a head start." Feena had grabbed her backpack, abandoning the box of crackers she'd hoped to smuggle onto the boat.

"This new friend of yours—" Lenore began.

"I really have to go, Mom."

But her mother had taken her arm, and Feena had seen the expression she knew all too well. Lately, unless Feena made a special effort, like Saturday night, when they'd stayed up in front of the Sony, watching horror flicks and howling like werewolves, Lenore looked more and more like Our Lady of Perpetual Sorrow. She wore this worried, disappointed face, and she whined when she talked.

"I'd like to meet her."

"What?"

"This new friend of yours, the one you've spent three out of the last six nights with"—*She'd been counting!*—"I'd like to meet her."

"Sure." Feena had made a mental note to pretend it was a different friend next time, though she didn't know which was more believable, making a best friend so fast or making so many! "I'll bring her over sometime."

Lenore retrieved the end of her sash, wrapped it around her waist. Without her makeup, she looked a little younger and a lot sadder. "I know this house isn't exactly the Taj Mahal," she'd said. "But I could find a cover for the couch. Get some of that peach swirl you like." She paused, hopeful. "For shakes?"

How long would it be before Our Lady of Sorrow turned into an angry detective prying? Spying? And how long could Feena go on lying to someone who, after all, cared about her more than anyone else on earth?

And now, here was Raylene, shouldering into her smock. It was always after five o'clock when she came back from work. "My mom's acting strange," Feena told her. "When do you get off?"

Raylene fixed Feena with a look that made her squirm. "When I get off," she said.

"It's just, she's getting kind of crazy with my never coming home."

"How about that?" Raylene's perfectly arched eyebrows arched higher. "Now, *my* mom, she's handling it real fine. She's only cried twice."

"Sorry." It seemed Feena was always saying that lately, or feeling it. "She wants to meet you. She told me today, she wants to invite you over."

Raylene laughed. "Well, now all we got to do is find someone to take care of Toffee while the three of us have tea."

Then, unpredictable as always, she relented. "I'll ask can I leave early." She kissed Christy, who, apparently under the impression he was going with her, had stood up and taken her hand. "And I'll look for a hat, maybe some baby shades for Toffee. We spent three hours in that sun yesterday."

"Three hours? And you didn't burn?" Feena looked at Raylene's gorgeous darkness, then turned away, embarrassed. "Well, I guess you don't, you can't—I mean..."

Astoundingly, Raylene was grinning, broad but warm. "Hey, have you ever had a black friend before?"

"Not exactly." *Friend,* Raylene had said. Not *acquaintance.* Or *classmate. Friend.* Feena smiled, too. "No," she said.

Raylene untwined her hand from Christy's and pushed open the cabin door. A broad stripe of light cut across the tiny room. "You're going to take some work, girl." She shook her head, still smiling. "You're going to take some serious work." And then she was gone, the cabin in shadow when the door swung shut.

The address in the paper turned out to be a turquoise doublewide in the Bide A Bit trailer court. The next day, while Raylene was watching Christy and it was her turn to go to school, Feena played hooky. She lacked Raylene's confidence about what they'd done, dreamed each night now of walking through a tunnel with glossy moss-slicked sides, of the walls collapsing in on her as she hurried toward a distant light.

The rumpled news clipping stuffed in her pocket had changed everything. It meant Christy's mother wanted him back. Feena needed to see for herself where they lived. Needed to know she was a rescuer. Not a kidnapper.

Bide A Bit looked like an endless parking lot. Mobile homes were lined up along gravel walkways, row after row, unrelieved by trees or hedges. Aside from two long-suffering, withered saw palmettos, one on each side of the entrance, Feena saw no hint of green. The sun beat off pebbles, off tarmac, off the steaming metal roofs of the trailers. Bide A Bit was right, Feena thought, searching the parched, shadeless rows. Bide A Bit and Get Out Quick!

There was a laundromat two trailers down from number ten, the address in the article. Feena sat out front on a bench, as if she were waiting for the spin cycle to end. She'd brought a book, and opened it now in her lap. Casual. Easy.

But she didn't read; she studied the vivid blue trailer instead. The paint was peeling off its aluminum sides, and a tin awning over the front windows had come unfastened on one end, letting in more sun than it kept out. Feena couldn't stop watching the place, as if each sordid detail, each crack and rust spot, confirmed the rightness of what she'd done. *Christy shouldn't live in a place like this.* Vindicated, self-righteous, she noted the lidless garbage can heaped to the brim, the torn candy wrappers and the bottles strewn across the narrow strip of asphalt that led to the door. *Anybody could see that.*

And hear it, too. Seconds after Feena sat down, a man inside the trailer started yelling. He must have been in a back room, because she couldn't see anyone through the front windows. But lord, she could hear his voice. Loud, angry, and strangely rhythmic—a rhythm Feena recognized. "You goddamn slut. You filthy whore. You stupid bitch." Again and again. The pink arms at Ryder's had risen and fallen to the same beat. Over and over.

And then the man she couldn't see—the invisible, angry voice—upped the ante. The flimsy trailer rocked on its cement foundation, or at least it seemed to Feena that everything—the angle of the door, the windows, the plastic flower pot on the stoop—changed, tilted when he started throwing things. Heavy things. She heard them hit the walls, break against the floor, and once there was a dull thud Feena didn't want to think about. Under it all, there was crying. A woman sobbing, begging him to stop.

She wasn't really surprised when Christy's mother opened the door, then slammed it behind her. There were no railings alongside the cinderblocks that served as steps, and in her rush, the pink-armed woman slipped on the last one. Without breathing, Feena watched, fascinated, as the woman lost her balance, then regained it. When she was steady, she turned, checking behind her as if she thought someone might follow her out the door. But the trailer was quiet, and suddenly Christy's mom was lurching toward the laundromat.

Feena froze. She buried her head in her book, waiting for the woman to walk past her and go inside. But instead, she sighed loudly and sat down beside Feena. She was wearing jeans, just as she had at Ryder's. There were dark bands around the armholes of her sleeveless shirt, and Feena smelled a not unpleasant mix of sweat and talc. "Jesus," the woman said, shaking her head and addressing no one in particular. "Sweet mother of Jesus, it sure is hot out here."

Feena pulled the book nearer, turned her head away. What if Christy's mother recognized her? What if she remembered her from Ryder's or the playground? She tried to focus on the paragraph in front of her, but the words ran together, seemed as meaningless as if they'd been written in another language.

The woman shifted sideways onto one broad hip and retrieved a pack of cigarettes from the pocket of her jeans. "What you reading?"

Feena coughed as the woman lit up. How had she gotten herself in this bind? Why hadn't she listened to Raylene? Why hadn't she run the minute Christopher's mother opened the door? "Just a book for English." She waved the paperback under the woman's nose, stood up, and looked toward the laundromat door.

"That's good," the woman told her. She ran a plump, lineless hand across her hair, no longer contained by the dolphin-shaped barrette that hung like an earring on one side of her head. She seemed unaware of the impression she must be making, the red face, the eyes swollen with crying. "I never finished school. Wish I did every single day that passes. You know?"

Feena nodded, then made an awkward break for the inside of the laundromat. "Yeah," she said, on the run. "Sorry, I have to get my stuff." She ducked through the door and stopped at the first dryer she found full. Foolishly, desperately, she opened it and began unloading some stranger's clothes, piling underwear and shirts on the top of the still-warm machine.

To her horror, Christopher's mother followed her inside, stood by the machine, talking and smoking, as if they were friends. "You live around here?" she asked in a voice that was much softer than the one Feena remembered from Ryder's.

It was impossibly hot and humid inside, with a dozen thrumming machines backed against windowless walls. Feena tensed, waiting for some sign of recognition, but clearly, the woman didn't remember her. Stuck in her role, Feena folded a man's undershirt, then began bunching socks in pairs.

"No," she said, trying not to look in the woman's eyes, keeping her face averted, down, away. "I'm just visiting." At least, she thought, grabbing for another sock, someone would be happy to find their laundry sorted. She only hoped they didn't come back to claim it now.

"Must be nice," the woman observed. "Not living in this dump." She handed Feena the mate to a faded pink sock she'd picked up. "If I'd finished school," she continued, "I could get outa here. Get a job somewhere. You know?"

Feena wished the woman wouldn't keep saying "You know?" Feena didn't know, and she didn't want to.

"My daddy used to tell me I was too thick to slice. Told me that right up till he got sick and needed me to dress him and feed him and wipe his ass." She watched Feena folding, folding. "Guess I was smart enough to do that, huh?"

Feena searched the room wildly, spotted an empty laundry basket on an oilcloth-covered table in the back.

"Before he got sick, Daddy used to spend his time knockin' sense into me and my sister." She sucked on her cigarette as if she were breathing air, slow and deep. "You know?"

Feena dashed for the basket, piled the clothes in.

"Yeah. He sure used to like slamming us around." The woman's voice didn't sound angry or even particularly excited. She could have been describing a wrestling match on TV. "Where you going?"

Feena was already at the door. She held the basket against her chest, and backed out into the sunlight. "Got to get this back," she explained, turning afterward, racing down the first path she came to, then out of the park.

She was blocks away before she felt the weight of the basket, realized she'd run off with someone's wardrobe. Next to what she'd already taken, that seemed a small offense. And she couldn't return the clothes now, not with Christopher's mother hiding out in the laundromat.

As she neared the boat, she slowed her pace. She had nearly five hours until she'd be able to slip into the cabin, drop her backpack on the table, and complain to Raylene about how lame math had been or how the cafeteria still figured Spanish rice was one of the four food groups.

She stashed the laundry basket behind a hedge of fat-faced clematis that bordered the parking lot where the girls phoned their mothers each afternoon. Then, resurrecting an old habit, she headed home. It had been years since she'd come to her mother with a "boo-boo," but suddenly, even though there was no visible wound, no place you could plaster a Flintstones Band-Aid, Feena needed Lenore.

fourteen

.

.

.

It was Friday and sometimes, Feena remembered, her mother came home to eat when her wallet was empty and her credit card was maxed. "The trouble with paychecks," Lenore always complained, "is they don't come twice a week."

It wasn't that Feena planned to tell her mother about Christy. Not exactly. But without the baby and the TV, it would be just the two of them. *That's my big girl*. The hairbrush stroking, stroking. *That's my big, good girl*.

But when Feena opened the door, the Pizza Hut was empty. It surprised her how disappointed she felt, how lost. She considered making herself lunch, but the heat that had built up, like a heavy animal waiting in the small rooms and leaping out at her as soon as she walked in, changed her mind. She settled for grabbing a can of soda from the refrigerator and the last stale doughnut from a box on the counter. She locked the front door behind her, then headed back for the boat.

Peter Milakowski, standing by the tugboat ride, waved at her as she hurried past. "Hey," he called, almost cheerfully. "You be careful they don't put you in jail."

Feena froze. *What did the old man know?* She walked to the park gate, and he waved again. *What could he possibly know?*

Now the wave turned into a summons. "So, come," he said. "You could hide here."

She stuffed the doughnut into her backpack and sauntered with as much indifference as she could to where he stood. "Why should I hide, Mr. Milakowski?"

"You don't study, they come to get you, right?" He turned and peered into the metal pool where the tugs rested, unmoving. "School, it makes you sick?"

Feena felt her whole body relax. She stood beside him for a second, savoring the relief, staring into the filmy water. "No," she said. "I have a free period, that's all."

They turned, almost in unison, and leaned their backs against the tub. The amusement park was suffering its lunchtime slump; there wasn't a single mother or toddler in sight. The two other rides were going through the motions, anyway, as if they carried baby ghosts. Around and around.

After a while, Mr. Milakowski roused himself. "Hmmm," he said. He reached his elegant, gnarled fingers into the tool belt he wore around his waist and retrieved a small bottle. He held the bottle over the water, emptying a few drops beside the nearest boat. "School makes me sick a lot of times also." He slapped at something, maybe a mosquito that couldn't tell time, then found his mental place again. "Only thing I like of school is Miss Marna."

"Your teacher?" Feena watched the water by the little tug turn a furious blue.

Mr. Milakowski nodded. "Miss Marna was for me an angel."

He flipped a switch that set the boats in motion and stirred the water to a gentle cerulean. "But she has no time for good boys, see? She is watching always bad ones. This," he added, talking above the noise of the motor that drove the boats, "is why Peter Milakowski becomes the worst student in the whole school."

They moved to the bench alongside the ride, a bench from which mothers could wave and call out as their sons and daughters sailed by. Mothers could do this, of course, only if the ride was working, and only if there were any children there to ride it.

"I am sure she likes the other boys better, see?" Mr. Milakowski pocketed the bottle, then crossed his skinny legs, resigned to this lull, to the empty park. "She makes them to sit by her. Right up front where they can see her angel's face.

"But not me. Never me." He looked at Feena now, and she tried to resurrect a little boy from the elderly man in stained khakis. "Those other boys," he said, "they always talk out. They make wrong answers.

"So I decide to help her notice Peter Milakowski. I start talking and I don't stop. And every answer I give is wrong." He smiled at the sixty-year-old memory as the tugs circled behind him. "I bite my tongue to keep the right ones down."

Feena was smiling, too. "Then what happened?"

"Miss Marna, she gives me a long, sad look. She says I am hopeless, the worst boy she ever knows. Then she asks I hold out my hands to get hit with her ruler. There are tears in her eyes when she counts ten hits." His face grew animated, warm with conviction. "And I move up."

"Up?"

"After, she sits me in the front row, right next to her desk. I sit there for all year long."

"And she really cried when she hit you?"

"Hmmmm," he said again. "When Miss Marna stops and I see tears in her eyes the color of wren's eggs, you know what I want?"

Feena shook her head.

"I want to move back to the last row. It hurts less than watching her cry."

It wasn't so hard, really, Feena decided now, to think of Mr. Milakowski as a boy.

But there was no comparison, she was sure. The sainted Miss Marna, who hit children in another time, another place, who cried when she wielded her ruler, who was worthy of a small boy's devotion. She couldn't have been anything like the strange red-faced woman Feena had just left standing by the dryers in the trailer park laundromat.

Still, even after she'd said goodbye to the old man and was headed back to the boat, she remembered the dangling barrette, the subdued, frightened voice. Yes, it was true. There *had* been tears in the woman's eyes. But what did that prove? There was that cigarette, too. The one she'd seemed grafted to, the one she'd used when she...Those tears didn't make Christy's mother an angel, Feena decided. They just made her someone who'd gotten as good as she gave. Didn't they?

When she reached the parking lot, she remembered the laundry basket she'd hidden there. She told herself she was only going to return it, that was all. But once she'd gone back to Bide A Bit and dropped off the basket, she couldn't leave. There was yelling in the trailer again.

She knew better than to sit out front now, so she stole around to the side street, where there was no chance she'd be seen.

This time, she could see them both through a window. Or rather, she could see their outlines through the half-closed blinds. What she noticed first was how the man (was he Christy's father?) towered over the woman. She had seemed robust and chunky next to her son, but she looked helpless beside the giant who held her arm while he yelled, virtually in her face.

After a while, he dragged her closer to the window. Feena ducked around the corner, then sneaked back in the middle of his tirade. "Three months," he screamed. "I been paying for this piece of junk for three lousy months." As he yelled, he pounded on something in front of them, just out of sight below the window frame. "And that ain't all, is it?" He yanked the woman's arm up and down as if it were a slot machine lever and he would hit the jackpot if he pulled hard enough. "Is it?"

The woman answered, but Feena couldn't hear what she said. Then the man let her go and lumbered to the other side of the room, coming back with a brightly colored box in his hand. "Goddamn computer game, for crying out loud. The kid ain't even three." He hurled the box toward the woman, who first tried to catch it, then settled for dodging as it sailed past her head.

"And this. What in hell you buy a treadmill for?" He kicked at something else outside the window frame.

"You ain't lost a pound in six years." He grabbed her again. "Fat bitch." He raised one trunklike arm and brought it down, pushing the woman into a wall. She collapsed like a plush doll, throwing her hands in front of her face, the same way Feena had seen Christy do. "Stupid, fat bitch. You gonna buy us right into the street, that's what."

He left her there and returned to pound whatever it was under the windowsill. "Right into the frigging street," he repeated, slamming down with a huge, balled fist, hitting it again and again. "Stupid whore." *Slam.* "Spending money I don't got." *Slam.* "Can't take care of your own kid." *Slam.* "Think you can waltz out"— *slam*—"and spend every lousy cent"—*slam*—"I god-damn make." *Slam.*

He stopped hammering, stepped backward when his last blow triggered a thin, mechanical sound—an ironic, bouncy Joplin tune that filled the room and spilled out the window. That was when Feena finally understood Christy's fascination with *Mama's Music.* And that was the moment, as the player piano spouted its canned repertoire, that his mother made her escape.

She was out the door and around the doublewide before Feena saw her coming. Then they were walking side by side, Feena trying to walk faster to leave her behind. "Hey." The woman reached for Feena's arm and hung on with the grip of a drowning swimmer. "Wait, will you."

But Feena didn't. She deliberately picked up speed, on the totally irrational theory that if she could just get in front, the woman would drop off and fall away, a racer acknowledging defeat.

"Listen, you gotta slow down." The woman was chugging along the gravel walk, her heavy footfall slower than Feena's, out of sync. "I need you to stay." Her voice trailed away, got lost in a flurry of breathless coughs. "Please!"

Feena slowed, turned.

"My old man," the woman said, stopping, inhaling as if the stifling air were food and she hadn't eaten for days. She turned, too, nodded toward the distant trailer, where a looming figure was standing on the steps, his eyes shaded under one hand. Although Feena couldn't be sure, there was something familiar about the way he stood, his size. "If he sees me with someone, he'll leave me alone. Please," the woman repeated.

Feena turned back but slowed down even more, until they fell into step together. Just as in the laundromat, anyone who didn't know, anyone who stumbled on them this way, would have assumed they were friends. *An afternoon jog,* Feena thought, furious with herself for having come back. *Just us girls.* Though it was obvious the woman had no idea who she was, Feena still kept her face averted, concentrating on the chalky stones under her feet.

"He don't dare touch me if there's witnesses," the woman told her, breathing easier now. "You know?"

That explained why she had rushed up to Feena last time, why she'd insisted on helping with the laundry.

"My name's Delores, Delores Pierson," the woman told her. "Who you visiting, anyway?"

Feena didn't even try to make up a lie. "Can't you call the police?" she asked.

"Huh?"

"Your husband," Feena said, blinking into the sun. "Can't you tell the police what he does to you?"

"The cops? What good would that do?" Delores Pierson didn't stop walking but glanced down the street behind them again.

Feena looked back, too. The trailer seemed strangely domestic from a distance. The cracks and dirt didn't show in the bright sun, only the red plastic begonia in the pot on the stoop. The man had disappeared from the steps.

"The cops don't do nothing," Delores said, turning back, walking more slowly now. "Last time I called, they come over and one of them puts their hand on my old man's shoulder. He talks real soft to him, real friendly. Then he looks at me. 'I know everything will be all right now,' he tells me. 'I know you both don't want more trouble.'

"Like it's my fault." She stopped, dug into her jeans pocket. When she came up empty, her voice broke.

"Like as long as I don't want trouble, I can keep my teeth in my head. You know?"

Feena wished there were laundry to pick up, a basket to grab, to rush off with.

"I'm gonna get out, though." Delores wiped her face, started walking again. "My cousin's gonna fix me up with a job in Atlanta. I'm heading up there soon as I get my kid."

Feena willed her face to stay frozen. "Your kid?"

They had gone the length of one side of the court, turned now to their left, and started down another. "Uh-huh." Delores's face was red with exertion, her arms and forehead glistened with perspiration. "Don't no one believe me, but they've taken my baby."

"'They'?"

"Kidnappers, that's who." Delores wrapped her arms around herself, slowing again. Her voice took on a singsong quality, as if she'd told this to herself over and over. "Ain't no other way Christopher would go and disappear. You know?

"I have him trained good. He knows to mind. And he knows to wait for me."

"You left him alone?" Something kept pushing Feena to the edge of safety, made her need to be sure. "All by himself?"

The singsong stopped, and the little girl was back in Delores's voice. "No," she said, "not for real. It's like a game we play. You know? I mean, sure, I tell him if he don't mind me, I'm leaving. But he knows that's only talk. He knows I ain't doing nothing but blowing steam.

"That's how come he wouldn't run off on his own. I know somebody's gone and took him. I looked everywhere. And my old man? He's been all over town, too. Only he don't half believe me hisself. You know?... Hey, wait. Where you going?"

Feena didn't want to hear any more. She wanted to be back with Christy and Raylene. She didn't wave this time, just took off as soon as she saw the trailer park gates. Took off and didn't look back.

Raylene was right; Feena saw that now. She never should have come here. Everything was confused, everything was worse, like a sore that starts to heal until some fool rips it open. Some fool named Feena Elizabeth Harvey. *Damn,* as Raylene would say. Just plain damn.

fifteen

.

.

.

She was back to keeping secrets. It had felt so good to have someone to come clean with, someone she could tell the whole story to. Now Feena was holding it all in again. She could never admit to Raylene that she'd been to the trailer court, much less that she'd actually talked to Christy's mother.

It was hardest at night, before one of them went home and the other settled down with the baby. That was the time when, more and more, the two girls talked. While Christy slept in the narrow bunk, they relaxed in the slow velvet space between afternoon and night, the time before the mosquitoes and no-see-ums set in. They sat in the benches on each side of the table, their voices low so as not to wake the baby, and compared notes—on books, on boys, on things Feena never dreamed she'd be able to share with anyone. Once, she'd even managed to tell Raylene about the dream she'd had. About how she'd watched Jane and Janie sail off on the old ship.

"Lord," Raylene had told her, chuckling. "As many times as I read those books, I never did picture the two of them in the same boat!" She shook her head. "That quiet, white-bread Jane." She'd grinned and looked almost sheepishly at Feena. "Don't get me wrong, now. I like Jane; it's just she's more of a thinker than a doer, see?"

Feena had nodded. She couldn't help loving the way Raylene talked about characters as if they were real people, someone she knew.

"And Janie? Well, it's almost like she figures thoughts would slow her down."

Feena had to admit, dreams didn't always make sense. "I guess it *is* pretty silly," she'd said.

"And the way they talk," Raylene went on. "Jane's words are so perfect, so beautiful, I figure she lies awake all night just cooking up what she's going to say next day." She'd laughed again, then, remembering Christy, lowered her voice. "Now Janie—everything she says, it has the Old South in it. She sounds just like my grandma."

"Well, I only—"

"Course," Raylene had interrupted, reconsidering the proposition she'd just rejected, "I guess they could spell each other some. I mean, Janie could set Jane straight every time she panics." She'd grinned then, as if she might have been joking all along. "And Jane, she could get a crazy idea once in a while that would start Janie thinking. Yeah, they might do all right, after all." Finally, that look of hers, that steady, no-nonsense look. "They just might pull it off, those two."

And didn't it take two? Feena not telling Raylene about her visits to the blue trailer—wasn't that like Jane holding out on Janie? What if she *was* thinking crazy? What if a single word from Raylene could set her straight, make her sane and sure? Each afternoon, when Raylene put down her orange soda, leaned back, and asked, "So, girlfriend, which way the world throw you today?" Feena almost told her, almost dumped her guilt, her confusion, in Raylene's lap. Like Christy with that smile of his: "Fix." But she didn't.

And if Raylene noticed a difference in Feena, the way she grew suddenly quiet when Raylene crowed about how happy the baby was, how much weight he was gaining, she never let on. Even though Feena stopped aiding and abetting her plans to sneak Christy into daycare when the "heat" was off, even though she no longer laughed when Christy did as he'd been taught and called Raylene "Mama Ween," Raylene seemed oblivious.

If Raylene hadn't fallen quite so effortlessly into the role of parent, things might have been different. If Feena hadn't missed home so much, hadn't begun to feel she'd forgotten what it was like to be a kid, the pressure might not have built up the way it did. And maybe if Raylene hadn't been over an hour late two weeks into their "split shifts," things wouldn't have gotten out of hand. Of course, then Feena would never have known. Never have guessed that a train could gather speed and come out of nowhere, crushing everything in its path. That she could look up in bewilderment and realize she was the train.

It started slowly. She was aware only that she had to light the lantern and that her mother would be wondering where she was. She noticed, too, that Christy was fussy, unusual for a child who took almost every setback and disappointment in stride.

He had spilled juice on one of his books, not *Mama's Music,* but another of his favorites. It had upset him, and he'd tried for minutes on end to rub the purple stain off the picture of a polar bear. He used a paper towel, as he'd seen Feena do the day before. Bent over the book, his face damp and determined, he scrubbed away until both the towel and the page threatened to dissolve into nothing.

He complained loudly when Feena swept up the book, just in time to save the bear from extinction. "Baa," he insisted. "Bear take baa."

"No, Christy," she'd told him. "The bear can't take any more baths. He's had enough." She put the book on a shelf out of his reach. "Let's let him dry."

But he continued to whine, looking constantly up at the shelf above him. "Baa?" he asked plaintively. "Mo baa?"

Feena, preoccupied, pushed him aside. "No, Christy. Not now."

He retreated for a minute, but then came back, his arms loaded with the cartons, spoons, and paper cups he used for building. "Pay," he announced. "Feen pay."

A large, feather-headed moth had fallen in love with the candle, Feena noticed, and was beating itself against the lantern grate. "No," she said, without looking at Christy. "I don't want to play right now." Where was Raylene, anyway? Had something gone wrong?

"Pay!" Christopher unloaded his building materials into her lap. "Want pay!"

She brushed the junk off her knees. "Take it away, Chris," she said. "Go play on your bed." Between the moth's persistent thumping and Christy's whining, Feena could hardly think. What would she tell Lenore? And how was she ever going to study for that geometry test? She found her backpack, took out the math text, but Christy's hand was on the page almost before she opened to it.

"Weed," he said, changing tack. "Feen weed."

"No." Still, she didn't look at him. "This isn't that kind of book. Raylene will read to you later, okay?"

"Ween," he told her now. "Want Ween." He brushed himself against her repeatedly, like the moth throwing itself at the light. "Want Ween! Want pay!"

Finally, Feena looked down at him. And suddenly his smallness, his dependence irritated her. *I'm not who you think I am. Stop looking at me like that.* "Don't you understand?" She moved him out of the way, so his shadow wouldn't fall across the book. "I can't play all the time."

He closed in again, an afflicted expression on his small features; he grabbed her hand and thrust himself back against her until the pressure of that slight body seemed almost unbearable. She wanted to bat it away just as she'd pushed the cartons and blocks out of her lap. His tiny hand in hers was too much—too hot, too moist, too heavy.

Feena's blood pumped into her head and hands. She felt tingly, as if one more touch would send her flying out of herself. But that small hand kept coming back.

When she actually lifted his fingers off hers and grabbed him by the shoulders, she felt lightheaded, powerful. "Don't you know I have other things to do," she told him, "other things to think about besides you?"

It must have been her stern tone. Or maybe the way she'd pushed him away from the book. Anyway, he started crying, sudden, silent tears that surprised them both. He stood his ground, though, dabbing at his eyes. "Pay!" he sobbed, indignant. "Feen pay!"

He hadn't napped all day, and it was well past his dinnertime. But Feena was beyond patience and excuses. She grabbed his shoulders again, turned his chin up so he'd have to see her, have to understand. "Didn't you hear what I just said?" His bones were like a kitten's or a bird's between her fingers. "What did I say, Chris?"

Christy's face, his angel's face, darkened then. Still crying, he shut his eyes and turned away from her. He put his arms around his head, crouched the way he had at the amusement park. He was protecting himself... from *her*! And why did the anger get worse then? Crawling into her throat like a meal she couldn't keep down? Why did Feena want to shake him, make him know she would never hurt him? *Make him stop. For god's sake, just make him stop!*

When Raylene opened the doors, when she raced into the cabin breathless, the newspaper in her hand, Feena and Christy were startled, as if they'd been wakened from a bad dream. The frustration, the exhaustion

Feena had felt seconds before got swallowed up in a rush of adrenaline, a shock she'd been expecting for so long, she leaned into it like a sharp wind. The headline was bannered across three columns: SECOND KIDNAPPING SPARKS DRAGNET. TWO CHILDREN MISSING AS POLICE COMB AREA.

"It was on the radio, too," Raylene told her, whispering as if Christy were asleep instead of hugging her knees, trying to pull her face down to his. "I heard it at work. Merilee, she's the manager, she keeps music on all the time, even when she's talking to you." She finally stooped down, kissed the baby absently, then waited impatiently for Feena to finish the article.

"The way I see it," she said, when Feena finally raised her eyes from the paper, "someone took another kid, and the brilliant police figure there's a kidnapper out there who can't quit." She plucked Christy up from the floor, sat him on her hip, and smiled grimly. "Like one of these won't give him trouble enough."

Feena said nothing, felt nothing. She sat still, waiting for the numbness to wear off.

"I saw three cop cars on the way here," Raylene told her. "They're all over the place."

"God." Feena felt dizzy now, short of air. It was as though they were trapped in a mystery novel or a film, as though they were living lives that didn't belong to them. She and Raylene were ordinary people; how could this be happening? "Do you think they'll find us?"

Raylene shook her head. "Cops don't want snake-bites any more than the rest of us. And if they use dogs, the water will throw them off the scent."

Feena couldn't believe it. "Are you actually suggesting we stay here?"

"Not forever. But it's as good a place as any till we figure how to deal."

"Deal?" Feena wanted to crumple up the paper, tear it into pieces. Instead she folded it back, stood up. "What do you mean, 'deal'? You read this, Ray." She remembered Christy's mother, how no one believed her. Now they would. "It's official. We're *kidnappers*. How do we deal with that?"

Christy, catching the tension, wriggled in Raylene's arms, began to fuss again. "Down!" he whined, reaching for the floor as if it were miles away. "Want down!"

Raylene set him on his feet, lowered her voice. "I don't mean we stay here forever. Just long enough to get our heads straight." Babyless now, she shrugged, opened her arms. "Then who knows? Maybe we could take a bus trip somewhere. Give them time to find that other baby and go back to checking parking meters."

Part of Feena hoped it could happen. Red shoes and magic wishes, a fairy-tale escape. "I wanted to rescue Christy as much as anyone," she told Raylene. "But what if it's not so easy? I mean, what if it hurts other people? What if she wants him back?"

"Back?" Raylene sat down, deflated. "What do you mean?"

"Look," Feena began, "I went to see Christy's mom." She put out a hand as if to defend herself when she saw Raylene's eyes catch fire. "I had to, Ray. I had to know we were doing the right thing.

"And I'm not so sure anymore. Yes, she's got a temper. But you would, too, if you lived the way she does."

"Which is?"

"Which is in a tiny trailer that's too small for the yelling and hitting that goes on there. I saw it, Ray. I didn't mean to, but I—"

"Lots of people have problems. That's no excuse."

"She wants him, Ray. She'll stay there and get beat up until she gets him back." Feena didn't mention what had happened a few minutes ago, but she remembered the feeling of Christy's bird bones, her own helpless anger.

The heat in Raylene's eyes hadn't cooled. "What? You think you can just up and return Toffee, like some toy you're tired of?

"Listen, girl, I didn't help you out so you could roll over and play dead just when he has a chance to start fresh. I plan to see he gets that chance." She glared accusingly at Feena. "Even if all you got in mind is to quit on him."

It wasn't that easy. Feena knew it wasn't. "What if," she said quietly, slowly, "he wants it, too?"

"What?"

"What if Christy wants to go home?" She remembered the baby pointing to the piano book, remembered his excited, triumphant shout. "Ma!"

Raylene didn't answer. She sat now, her head bent forward on her slender neck, as if she were thinking over what Feena had said. Then, in the slice of stillness between their squabbling, the thunder hit. First there was a deep, throaty rumble, and the next second, the storm was on top of them, rattling in the sky like a steel ball hurled down the world's longest bowling alley.

Christy screamed. It was the first time Feena had been with him during a Florida downpour, and she was suddenly helpless in the face of his panic. "Shhh," she said, stooping down, picking him up off the floor he'd begged for just moments before. "It's all right. Shhh."

But he howled louder, covering his ears with his hands each time the thunder struck, his face contorted, purple. Instinctively, Feena looked across to Raylene, and just as naturally, Raylene took the baby from her. She held him against her shoulder, his face nestled there like a tiny infant's, then she began to walk the floor with him. She sang in the same sweet sunset voice Feena had heard at the old restaurant. Low and croony, slow and thick as liquid glass, finding a shape all its own in the middle of the storm.

Christopher quieted, and Raylene looked over her shoulder at Feena. "I'm not asking you again," she said.

177

"I'm just telling you, Toffee deserves a chance. Same as all of us. Okay?"

Feena nodded.

"And don't go doing anything crazy till we talk this out." She stared hard at Feena. "Promise?"

Feena nodded again.

sixteen

.
.
.

All next day, Feena was in school, but out of body. During history, she forgot about the Yalta conference and remembered that albatross she'd seen in the nature film on TV. A dumb bird in love with a plastic decoy. In algebra, she thought about her mother, mad for the soaps, and about Peter Milakowski, with a crush on a teacher he hadn't seen in sixty years. At lunch, alone at a table of seniors, she nearly cried for Christopher, devoted to a woman who didn't even know how to love him back. And cutting across the soccer field after eighth period, heading toward the boat, she felt sorry for herself, too. For Feena Harvey, still in love with a baby who had died before he was old enough to know her name, still yearning for a father who had clearly forgotten her, turning him into some kind of hero from a novel.

What good was all that one-way love, anyway? All that yearning and flapping and waiting? It was like a plug with no socket, or one left-handed glove at the back of the closet shelf. Good for nothing, that's what it was.

That night, curled next to the baby, Feena dreamed that he was climbing a steep set of stairs. She kept stumbling after him, throwing her arms around his legs, trying to pull him down to her. But he was stronger than she was, and he moved higher and higher, not even looking back when she called his name.

Next morning a typical Florida sky, cloudless and unrelentingly blue, was waiting for them by the time Christy was awake and fed. The two of them opened the cabin door and stood on deck, blinking in the sun. Feena had put one of Raylene's headbands on the baby, combing out as many of the ringlets as she could, so that his hair hung straight and pale over his shoulders.

She hoped anyone who was looking for Christopher would be thrown off by the long hair and dress. And she hoped Raylene would forgive her for breaking her promise. After all, it was Raylene who had said Christy should have a vote, wasn't it?

She saw no patrol cars and no suspicious loiterers as they slipped through the woods along the dirt path, then walked the six blocks to the trailer park. It had been nearly three weeks since Christy had been home. If he wanted to go back, Feena would be able to tell, she was sure she would. And if he was afraid, if he cried or clung to her, turned his face away, why, then she'd know what that meant, too. She'd know he'd had enough. Enough slaps and kicks to last a lifetime.

When they reached the entrance, she felt him stiffen in her arms. He raised his head, kept turning around as if he were trying to catch a scent. At the turnoff to the gravel path that ran to the trailer, he bent from his waist like a jacknife, strained toward the ground. She put him down and let him walk the rest of the way.

The relief was familiar, like something she'd known would happen all along. And the regret, too. As Christy spotted the blue doublewide, he tried to break free of her hand and run. "Ma," he said, not looking at Feena—his eyes, his open-mouthed smile, his excited body, all turned toward the shabby trailer. "Want Ma."

She'd picked him up, feeling sick, wondering what to do next, when she heard the car behind her. It overtook them, and she saw the gold crest on its side.

Even though the driver was in plain clothes, Feena knew a police car when she saw one. As it nosed up the gravel road past them, then into the trailer's driveway, she tugged Christy into the laundromat, her heart pounding.

The detective climbed the steps to the trailer, and Delores Pierson, cigarette in hand, opened the door. In the seconds before she let the policeman in and closed it behind them, Feena changed her mind a thousand times. First, she decided to wait, to stay and explain things to the baby's mother, and to the officer, to give Christy up and turn herself in. Next, she was certain that would be a mistake, that the police might not let Christy live at home, that he'd end up in an orphanage or a foster home or wherever kids were sent when they had no place to go.

But if her brain was divided, her heart knew what it wanted. The instant the door closed, as if it were the starting signal for a race, Feena tore off with Christy, streaking out of the park gates and running through the woods.

She didn't stop until they were nearly back at the boat. They were coming out of the woods when she heard voices in the turnoff, saw the two police cars pulled up beside the phone booth. She didn't know what it was Christy was about to say, what he wanted to ask, but she clapped her hand over his mouth and, her footsteps sounding like padded drums, headed back the way they'd come.

The playground would be too dangerous, and even the library seemed risky. (What if the librarian had told the police about the strange orphan girl with no identification? Ryder's, the scene of the first "kidnapping," would certainly be crawling with police. Suddenly, she'd run out of safe places, and Raylene's idea of getting away didn't sound as silly as it had a few hours ago.

There were two problems, of course. Feena couldn't drive, and she didn't have any idea where she would go if she could. She had spent her summer in the old Chevy with the gearshift in park, not exactly a geographic adventure.

"A bus trip." Wasn't that what Raylene had said? Was it too late? Instinctively, she headed for the CVS, where Raylene was still at work. Yes, it was near the playground, but if they were careful, if she and Christy waited behind the store in the parking lot, they could catch Ray when she left.

A man came out the back door of the CVS, just as they got close. A boy a few years older than Christy rode on his shoulders, one hand around the man's neck, the other waving a small white prescription bag. The boy, flushed and giggling, wore a cardboard clown hat and kicked the man's chest with his heels. "Faster! Faster!" he yelled.

"*Bwu*," Christy announced, waving excitedly at the boy's hat. "Got *bwu*."

Feena scanned the playground and parking lot for police cars and slowed her pace. "Yes," she acknowledged, kneeling beside him, keeping one arm around his waist. The cone-shaped party hat, its foil trim glinting in the sun, was indeed blue.

"Pay!" Christy whooped now, reaching toward the boy, whose horse father had crossed the parking lot and was galloping in the direction of the playground. "Want pay!"

"No, Christy." Just for a second, Feena glanced back toward the CVS, hoping, however unreasonably, that Raylene had read her mind and would suddenly materialize at the door. Unfortunately, a second was all Christy needed.

He had broken her grasp before she knew it and was running joyfully, arms wide, toward the playground. "No!" she called, standing, racing after him. "Wait!"

He didn't. He careened after the boy and his father, crossing the parking lot, heading toward the sandbox where he'd played with Angel. But he never reached it. A man in uniform intercepted him, kneeling down to say something Feena couldn't hear, then standing to take his hand.

As if in slow motion, Feena saw Christy point in her

direction, saw the policeman gather him into his arms and come toward her. And then, like a nightmare unfolding, she saw another figure behind them both. He was almost as tall as the swings—a giant of a man who stood just as he had last week, his hand shading his eyes. It was the same man she'd seen on the steps of the blue trailer. The yelling man.

Trapped, Feena stayed where she was. Without Christy, she had no reason to run. "You lose something?" The officer smiled as he crossed the lot, then lowered Christy to the sidewalk. Squirming happily, the baby tugged at the policeman's hand, pulling him toward Feena.

Feena, doing what came naturally—what she would do even if it meant going to jail—held out her arms. Like a magnet slipping in place, Christy ran into them.

"How old is she?" The officer had brown eyes, only a little deeper than his uniform.

"What?"

"Little Miss Cutie Pie." He nodded at Christy, whose sweet face looked like a porcelain doll's under the headband. "How old is she?"

Feena willed the policeman to turn around, move on, get an urgent call on his beeper. "Three," she told him, remembering the paper had said two.

"Cute as a button." The officer folded his arms, obviously in no hurry, and smiled down at Christy.

"Cute as a little button." Behind the policeman, the oversize man from the trailer had seen something that caught his attention and was moving toward them.

"You baby-sitting?"

"Yes." Feena tightened her grip on Christy. Had the yelling man recognized them? Or was he only after the policeman? "I should get her home now." She turned away, then back. "Thanks a lot."

"I thought maybe you two were sisters." The policeman's shoulders, his perfectly pressed shirt, hid only part of the big man, who was now waving at them, yelling something Feena couldn't catch, didn't want to. "You look like you could be. Anybody ever tell you that?"

"No." The man had nearly closed the distance between them. Despite his sequoialike bulk, he was moving fast, his shadow stretched out behind him in the dusty baseball diamond that bordered the parking lot. "Hey!" he shouted in a voice Feena remembered all too well. "Wait up!"

"I really have to go," she told the officer. "Thanks again."

"Hey! Hey, wait up!" This time the policeman heard, turned toward the playground, and as he did, Feena knew she had only one chance. She picked Christy up, moving as quickly as she could without running. That was one thing she'd learned from her mother's TV shows: Don't run. They know you're guilty if you do. And they can always run faster.

The two men were talking, Christy's father looming over the policeman, when Feena reached the door to CVS. That was when she heard it. "Feena!" She turned wildly, like a cornered animal, and saw the battered car that had pulled up in the lot beside them. "Feena Harvey," Mr. Milakowski shouted. He was wearing glasses, clutching the steering wheel with both hands, holding on to it as if it were a life raft. "You should get in. Time to go home."

Feena stayed where she was, stunned.

"We need to hurry," the old man told her. He had stopped his sedan opposite the yelling man and the policeman, blocking her from their view. "You must get in now."

But Feena stood frozen as the officer stepped around from behind the car and put his hand to the brim of his cap. He smiled at Mr. Milakowski. "You know this young lady, sir?"

Peter Milakowski smiled back, nodding, as Feena remained paralyzed. "This is my granddaughter," he told the policeman. He took one hand off the wheel to open the passenger door for Christy. As he did, the big man loped over to the car, too.

"Sorry, we must go now." Mr. Milakowski was rolling up his window while Feena pushed Christy onto the front seat, got in herself, and closed the door. "We are already very much late."

With the yelling man beside him, the policeman spread the fingers of one hand wide and rapped smartly on the window with the other. He looked suddenly stern, impatient. Mr. Milakowski glanced at Feena, put a finger to his lips, then rolled the window down again.

As the officer leaned into the opening, one arm across the bottom of the window, the yelling man tapped his shoulder. "Excuse me," he said. His respectful tone surprised Feena, but she saw the way he looked over the policeman's shoulder, the way his eyes swept the inside of the car. "Excuse me."

"I told you, I'll be with you in a minute, sir." The policeman turned around and stared at the yelling man. "All right, sir?" He cut the last word short, nearly spitting it out. Then he turned back, leaned through the window again. "Better get a seat belt for Cutie Pie," he told Mr. Milakowski. "That's no safe way to ride, okay?"

"Dwive," Christy begged, reaching across Mr. Milakowski for the steering wheel. "Want dwive."

"Sure, officer. Sure." The old man nodded, patting Christy's hands, smiling like a toothpaste ad. "I get a belt." He rolled up the window once more, then pulled out of the parking lot.

When Feena looked through the rear window, she saw the big man talking animatedly to the policeman;

the officer, his arms folded, his head bent, seemed to be communing with the asphalt. The traffic light turned green, and Mr. Milakowski made a left onto the highway, driving, Feena noticed, considerably faster than the speed limit.

seventeen

•

•

•

Police," Mr. Milakowski told her as
they drove. "They come around today, asking questions. I tell them I don't see anything."

"But how?..."

"I don't tell I find a plastic spoon and an old bottle
of baby food where golf clubs should be," he continued, squinting at the road. "I don't say I remember
you ask about hitting. But I put two and three
together, see?"

Feena nodded, amazed.

"I come to the drugstore for my heart pills, then I
see you with this baby. And I see police."

"Thank you." There was nothing else to say. Nothing more or less. Mr. Milakowski's car was a mess inside. The leather seats were prickly with rips; there were wads of tissues and empty paper cups on the floor. Feena had never been so glad to be anywhere in her life. "Thank you."

"In Poland," the old man told her, "the police come to school one day. They take Miss Marna. I never see her again."

They rode in silence for a few blocks, the blood red of poinciana trees flying by along the street, the corded banyons in between like hoary giants. "I don't ask questions," Mr. Milakowski said at last. "I don't tell you what to do."

Feena looked at the old man's profile, the nose that had surrendered to gravity, the withered skin. "I don't know what to do," she said. "I wish I did."

"Maybe nobody knows," he told her. "Maybe they do the best they can. What their heart says, yes?" He didn't turn to look at her, but his voice softened. "I drive you home now."

Feena felt the fuzzy top of Christopher's head under her chin and remembered the way he'd run toward the trailer, tipsy with happiness. The way he'd made the word *Ma* sound like a joke, a song, a present. It wasn't *her* heart that should make the choice; she knew that now. Quickly, before she could take it back, she asked, "Could we take Christy home first?"

She gave Mr. Milakowski directions to Bide A Bit, then hugged the baby closer, knowing—in the same half-conscious way you sometimes know you're happy—that she was about to lose something she could never get back.

Perhaps that was why she was able, afterward, to remember the last mile of the drive so well, to recall exactly how Christy felt and looked in her arms—how his damp hair clung together in fine springy curls, how his neck tasted of salt, how his fingernails were so small and dirty she could hardly bear it.

The trailer's driveway was empty when they pulled up. The police car had gone, and the yelling man was probably still combing the parking lot. Surely, he'd been after the patrolman, not Feena or a little girl in a patchwork dress. Cautiously, she took Christy's hand and opened the car door. Mr. Milakowski nodded, so she'd know he would wait for her. He was only a skinny old man, but that nod made her feel suddenly safer, surer about what she had to do.

She scanned the gravel road, then let the baby drag her up the concrete steps. This time when Delores Pierson opened the door, there was no cigarette in her hand. For a fraction of a second, she smiled at Feena, but then she spotted Christy. The headband and the dress didn't make any difference at all. She surrounded him, swallowed him in those vast arms. "Lord!" she said, her eyes closed while

Christopher kicked and laughed in her grasp. "Oh, dear lord in Heaven!

"Look at you!" She set him on her hip, put her chunky index finger on his nose. "What kind of getup is that, anyway?"

"Ma," Christy chortled. "Ma."

"Sweet Jesus, where are my manners?" Delores asked Feena, still cradling Christy. "Come on in!" She stood aside for Feena without letting him go. "If I was any happier, I'd be dead!" She patted Christy's hair, his arms, his legs. "I can't believe it; I just can't believe it. Where'd you find my baby?"

For one giddy minute, it seemed possible. Feena could lie, couldn't she? She could say she'd stumbled on the baby somewhere, the playground or the street. She would have remembered Delores was missing a child, would have brought him here. It was all perfectly logical, perfectly simple. She could drive home with Mr. Milakowski, feeling like a good citizen. Clean hands. A fresh start.

But something brave and foolish welled up in her, something borrowed from Raylene, maybe. Or Janie Woods. "I didn't find him," she told Christopher's mother. "I took him."

"What?" Delores said it lightly, humorously, as if Feena were telling a joke.

"I took him," Feena repeated. She peered over Christy's head into the littered living room. "Can I still come in?"

193

Delores's face changed, hardened, but she nodded toward the inside of the trailer, and Feena stepped past her into the dark room. The whir of an air conditioner and the sound of a TV grew louder as Feena wound her way around end tables and ottomans, a porcelain cat with gold eyes, a teacart with chrome wheels, and, of course, the player piano. Feena had never seen so many things crammed into such a small space. It looked as if Christy's mother was storing up for the world's biggest garage sale.

"What do you mean, you took my kid?" Delores, waving Feena toward the couch, perched on a tapestried love seat, Christy on her lap. He settled into his mother's bulk, a little sultan on cushions. He seemed dazed but happy, like someone who'd just given a huge party and was waiting for company to leave.

For the second time, then, Feena told the whole story. How she'd watched the two of them at Ryder's. How she'd walked off with Christy when his mother had driven away. How she'd played with him, read to him, loved him. How she'd only meant to help. How she could still help—she would baby-sit, take Christy to the library, the playground, give his mother a break anytime she needed it.

"Just what are you after?" Delores narrowed her eyes, held Christy tighter. "You aim to tell the case-worker about this?"

"Of course not." Feena wished the TV weren't so

loud; it was hard to hear herself over the noise. "Will you tell the police?" She glanced above Delores's head to a cluster of gilt frames on the wall. Each one held a print of a child ballerina with oversize doll's eyes. Each dancer was in a different pose. "I mean, about what I did?"

"I get it." Delores relaxed, her face softened. "Sure, sure. I won't go to the cops if you don't go running to DYFS. Deal?"

Feena relaxed, too, lowered her gaze again to Delores's face. She saw a look there, a hunger that gave her leverage. "There's just one more thing," she said.

"Yeah?"

"I meant what I said about helping." Feena hoped Delores couldn't see how much she needed this. "I'd really like to see Christy again."

At the sound of his name, Christy rallied from his contented stupor. He wriggled in his mother's arms. "Feen," he said, stretching his precious, dirty hands toward her. "Want Feen."

"Well, I don't need nobody watching over my shoulder every minute." Delores put the baby down, then grinned at her visitor. "But I sure wouldn't mind bein' able to go shopping sometime. That would be real nice. If you're sure you're not going to DYFS?"

Feena nodded. And if she had any doubts about bringing Christy home, they were erased as Christy's mother chattered on. She said she would tell the police she'd found him at a neighbor's; that was easy. She would get her old man to lighten up, too. Now that the baby was back, things would be normal again. And of course Feena could visit. So long as she didn't go to DYFS or the cops, she could come by every week. Regular as clockwork. Starting first thing on Saturday. "That'll be real nice," Delores told Feena. "Give me time to get my hair done, stuff like that. Like being rich and having a live-in. You know?"

And no, she promised, she would never hurt Christy again. Of course she wouldn't. It was just stress, but things were different now. Her old man was back on the day shift, so he wouldn't be lying around with nothing to do but complain. Sure, she would quit smoking; she had been intending to all along. The time hadn't been right, that's all. But now it was. Now everything would be better. Everything would be fine.

And as Christy scrambled into her lap, Feena allowed herself to picture it all coming true. Christy would have more people who loved him, more people who cared. It made perfect sense. Feena wouldn't have to give him up, she could still be part of his life. She could even take him home, show him off to her mother. He would love those flamingo glasses!

So there was no reason to cry, Feena knew, when Christy fell asleep in her lap. When his head slipped against her chest, his lashes making blue shadows on his cheeks. No reason to cry when it was time to hand him over, time to kiss his head and unwrap her hair from his

fingers, strand by careful strand. But they happened anyway, the tears. And the cold hard ache as she watched
his mother carry him away. "Good night, Christy," she
whispered, even though he couldn't hear her. "Sleep
tight."

True to his word, Mr. Milakowski didn't ask any questions on the ride back, just dropped her home as Lenore
was pulling up in the Chevy.

"Hey!" Feena's mother called as the old man drove
away. "Thanks a lot." She waved after his car, then
handed Feena a paper bag. "Just in time." She grabbed
another bag and led the way inside. "I got Mexican.
You staying?"

Lenore had apparently adjusted to the pattern—
every other night now, Feena was away from home.
But not anymore. The relief surprised Feena, the light-
bodied, free feeling. Not anymore. "Mom?" She followed her mother into the kitchen.

"Yeah? Better put that down; it's dripping."

"I have something to tell you."

"Sure. But let's eat first, okay?" Her mother got out
forks and glasses, laid the Styrofoam take-outs on the
table. "I had to drive to the moon for this stuff; it's
probably cold already."

So they both ate while Lenore drank. Feena had
tried to stop her from putting the wine out, but there
was something her mother wanted to celebrate. She

even poured Feena a token sip, then insisted on their clinking glasses. "It's not a big deal, of course," she said. "But a raise is a raise. Right?"

"Right." Feena, hungrier than she'd been in days, tore into the lukewarm frijoles, then watched with a kind of hopeless resignation as her mother grew less happy and more morose with each sip. Soon, the raise was forgotten, and what took center stage was a long list of grievances. "I'm supposed to be thrilled," Lenore asked her chicken enchilada, "because the department finally decides they're going to pay me for half the work I do?" She sawed away at her food with the wrong edge of a plastic knife. "This is supposed to make my cup run over?"

"Well, they must like what you're doing, Mom."

"Maybe, yeah," Lenore said. "I guess it's a good thing somebody somewhere appreciates me."

Feena, debating a second helping, ignored the warning flares and fell into the trap. "What do you mean?" she asked.

"I mean you; that's what I mean." Lenore studied the wine in her glass, letting it slide along the sides as she spun the stem in her fingers. "I mean you can't even stand to be home, and I guess I don't blame you."

Her mother's head got so low, Feena could hardly hear her. "I don't like being stuck with me any better than you do."

"What?" Feena sat up now, pushed her plate away. "Are you serious?"

"New house. New state. New job," Lenore said. "Same old me."

Feena hated this, really hated it. "Mom——"

"Same old dream every night."

"What are you talking about?" She was looking at the top of her mother's head now, the place where the purple streak started.

"There's this long tunnel," Lenore said, studying something in her lap. "It's black, darker than hell." She spoke in a monotone, as if she were reciting something she knew by heart, something that had lost its power to surprise her. "Christy's there; your brother's there at the end, and I'm walking toward him. He's just a baby, right?" She looked up now, through Feena rather than at her. "But he knows me, knows who I am. And when I get closer, he lifts up his little head and cries."

Feena, who had never heard her mother sound so soft, sat spellbound. Who belonged to this quiet hollow voice?

"I don't pick him up," Lenore told her. "I just stand there while he cries louder and louder. Finally I can't stand it, and I start yelling at him. 'Shut up,' I say. 'Shut up,' as loud as I can. 'Will you just shut up and let me get some sleep!'"

"Mom——"

"And then it's quiet." Lenore set her glass down, still staring past Feena. "Suddenly, it's so quiet." Her shoulders shook, but her gaze was clear, as if her body were crying but not her eyes. "I'd give anything if I could hear him, just once more. I'd lie down and die, honest to god. If he'd just wake up, if he'd just start bawling." She'd taken off her glasses and now she put her head in her hands. Feena couldn't see the tears, but she heard them.

"Mom, it's okay." Feena stood and put her arms around her mother. "It's all right. Everyone gets mad."

In between the sobs, gulping out the words. "He was afraid of me."

"I know," Feena told her. "We're all afraid of people we love." She laughed. "I'm afraid of you."

Lenore pulled back, mascara ringing her eyes. She looked at Feena hopefully. "Really?"

"Really." For the second time in a matter of weeks, they'd changed roles. They stayed like that for a moment, Feena holding her mother, stroking her hair, noticing among the purple and brown, some streaks of gray. *Gorgeous, Feen. You've got gorgeous hair.*

It was Lenore who pulled away, who stood and walked into her bedroom. Feena watched her mother open the bottom drawer of the dresser, get down on her knees, sniffing, and fumble through whatever was squirreled away there. When Lenore brought the box of photos back with her, setting them on the couch like an offering, Feena felt a little Christmas thrill run through her.

They hadn't looked at them in years. Side by side, with no TV blaring in the background and with the good strong light from a desk lamp Feena carried in from her room, they passed the pictures back and forth. In one, Feena's brother was, if not exactly sitting, propped at a sagging right angle in a green baby chair. On each side of him, holding a hand apiece, were Feena and her father, grinning like fools. In another, Feena was leaning over the baby, tickling him, not with her hands, but with long, dangling locks of her red hair. In others, Christy was alone, resplendent in baby fat and sparse blond hair, crawling, lying, kicking, even tear-stained and howling directly into the camera's eye.

It was a while before Feena noticed something missing. "Where were *you*, Mom?" she asked, forgetting. "Why aren't you in any of these?"

Lenore laughed. "Who do you think took them?" She was leafing through the faded shots, looking for something. "Here," she said at last. "Here's my favorite." She handed it to Feena, who saw herself at four, naked to the waist, the baby cradled in her arms.

"You were trying to nurse him, Feen. Isn't that something?" Her mother's voice was warm, admiring.

Feena looked again at the picture. The little girl's eyes were cast down, Madonna-like, toward Christopher, who obligingly nuzzled her flat, milkless chest. His face wasn't visible in the photo, just the clutching fingers. She shivered, shook off the tiny shadow hands that pressed suddenly, like warm breath, against her skin.

"Mom?" Feena put the picture on the coffee table and turned to Lenore. "Can I tell you something?"

Lenore nodded. Then while she stacked the rest of the photos in her lap, cupping them there as though they needed warmth, Feena told her mother everything. About the other Christy, who looked the way her brother might have; about his mother; about Raylene and cutting school; about Mr. Milakowski and the police. She didn't stumble over her words the way she had with Raylene. Telling Lenore was different, she realized, easier somehow. And she wondered, watching the lamplight frame her mother's head and hands, bleach the lines from her face, why she hadn't done it sooner.

"All that love," Lenore said when Feena finished. "You had that inside all this time." Her cheeks were still smudged with mascara tears, but she was smiling. "And you're sure she's going to quit smoking?"

"Yes."

"And hitting?"

"No hitting."

"She means it?"

"You should have seen them together, Mom. I tried so hard to make him happy, but all she had to do was"—she remembered Christy on his mother's lap—"just *be*."

"God, Feen, why did I go and move us to Florida?" Lenore touched her daughter's hands shyly, handling them as if they were brand-new, as if they were a baby's. "We could have been warm any damn where."

When the doorbell rang, they were both startled. It was the first time Feena had heard that strident, ugly bleat. She hadn't even known the Pizza Hut came equipped with anything besides the brass knocker, a horse's head that hung, beyond the reach of any but the tallest guests, on the peeling front door.

Outside, in air only slightly warmer than the living room, their visitor stood with one hand on her hip, her eyes telegraphing outrage. "Seems to me, you got some explaining to do," Raylene said.

eighteen

The fact of Raylene—her graceful frame, her angry face—at their door stunned Feena. Her friend seemed wrong here, out of place, smaller. "How did you know where I live?"

"They told me at school. I said you were craving your homework." Raylene folded her arms. "Are we going to talk out here?"

Feena stepped back from the door, just the way Christopher's mother had made room for her earlier. Raylene brushed past without a word. "How are you, Mrs. Harvey?" she asked Feena's mother in her best white-girl imitation. "I've been hoping to meet you for some time." She smiled broadly and took Lenore's hand. "And I guess you've been pretty curious about who Feen's been spending all her time with, right?"

Lenore, of course, was charmed. She offered Raylene leftover Mexican, got a flamingo glass out of the cupboard. Soon the two of them were seated at the kitchen table, chatting as though they'd known each other forever.

"You don't have to do that, you know," Feena said from the couch by the TV. (The kitchen table had only two chairs, and she didn't want to watch Raylene's company act, anyway.)

"What do you mean?" Raylene put down her flamingo glass, stared at Feena.

"I mean," Feena explained, "I've already told her."

Raylene looked incredulous. "Everything?"

"Everything."

"Well, that's fine, then." There was the vestige of a smile on Raylene's face as she pushed aside her plate, stood up from the table, and walked into the living room. "Maybe you could share some of that 'everything' with me." Then the smile vanished, along with her polite voice and talk. Her hands were back on her hips. "What have you done with Toffee?"

When Feena explained, when she told how Christy's mother had promised not to go to the police, how she was going to take better care of Christy, how she was even going to let them baby-sit (Feena didn't see any point in not including Raylene, even though she'd never mentioned her to Christy's mother), Raylene laughed. "And you believe her?" she asked. "Just like that, the slate's clean?"

"She loves him, Ray. I know she does."

"*Love*'s a word." Raylene shook her head. "I can't believe you took Toffee back there." She looked to Feena's mother for confirmation. "Did she tell you that baby was burned?"

Lenore nodded.

"What makes you God here, anyhow?" Raylene asked, turning back to Feena. "I thought you promised we'd decide this stuff together."

"He wanted to go home," Feena told her. "You didn't see him; you weren't there."

"I wasn't there because I was fronting for you. But I was there when you needed to drag your sorry ass to school. I was there when you had to go home and spend time with—" She stopped, remembering where she was, who was listening. "I was there when it counted, wasn't I?"

"Yes." There were tears in Feena's eyes, but she brushed them away before they could spill over.

Raylene walked closer to where Feena sat on the couch. "Seems like you owe me some," she said, unrelenting. "Seems like you got no cause to take that woman's word before mine."

"He was so happy when he saw her," Feena insisted. "All squirmy and wiggly like a puppy."

Raylene's hands were back on her hips. "Don't you know anything, girl? If you grow up in dirt, you love dirt. Is that reason to send him back?"

When Lenore spoke, it surprised them both. "Give her a chance," she said. At first Feena was grateful, thought her mother was taking her part, but Lenore was defending someone else.

"That's what this is, you know. A second chance." Feena's mother talked slowly, carefully, staring steadily at Raylene. There were tears in her eyes, but she let them brim over, run down her face. "Sure, I mean for you two. Who needs to be charged with kidnapping? But I mean for someone else, too."

"Not everyone's a natural mother; it's hard for some of us." She lowered her head for a second, then raised her eyes again, her features set like stone in the effort not to look away.

"We make mistakes; we get tired; and all the time there's this image of the perfect mother in our heads. You know, this mother with a capital *M*? This patient, selfless, wise saint? And every day, every minute, we're measuring ourselves against that picture, and we're saying, 'I can't do it. I can't be it.'"

"Mom—" Again Feena felt as though her mother were a child, wanted to hold her back, keep her out of hurt's way. But of course, it was too late for that.

"And the sad thing is, we don't always get another shot." Lenore smiled at Raylene now, a thin, underwater smile. "What I'm saying is, if you plan on growing up to be perfect adults, then get right back there and take that woman's baby away from her quick. Before she gets upset. Or exhausted. Or just wants some time to herself.

"But if you figure you might get impatient yourselves sometime, might want to scream or lash out or just plain run away, then maybe you ought to let her try again. And maybe you can be there for her when things get rough."

For once, Raylene had no ready answer. Her eyes dropped away from Lenore's. And in the silence that followed, Feena knew Christy's mother would get her second chance. She forced herself to concentrate on the memory of Delores's huge arms holding Christy, tried to blot out the images of their beating him, burning him, pushing him away.

Feena hated waiting a whole week. But she'd agreed not to visit Christy until next weekend. "To give the old man time," his mother had said. "Let him get used to having a kid around again."

And there were compensations. While she counted the days, marking them off like a prisoner in a cell, there was school—school with a difference. Now, instead of alternating days, she and Raylene attended

Washanee together. No longer wandering the halls in a lonely, protective daze, Feena was surrounded by Raylene and her crew. Like a proud, noisy wave, they buoyed her up, swept her along with them. Instead of eating lunch alone, Feena found herself at one of the loudest, most sought-after tables in the cafeteria.

Once she glanced up and saw Nella Beaufort staring at her from across the room. As soon as their eyes met, Nella nudged someone else at her table, pointing in Feena's direction. Her face rearranged itself then, a small frown furrowing her brows—pity, maybe, or disapproval. But it was too late. Feena had already seen the hungry look that came first. The raw need to be liked, to be chosen, to have a life.

Feena knew, of course, that her own acceptance by the movers and shakers hadn't happened because she'd lost four pounds or developed a sparkling personality overnight. It was because she was a friend of Raylene's, because every so often, in the middle of a diatribe against assigned seating or salsa that tasted like tomato juice, Raylene would stop, would nudge Feena's shoulder for confirmation. "Right, Feen?" she'd ask, and the thrill was always new, always astonishing.

Sometimes, in the center of that charmed group, the smart words and the smooth moves cradling her, Feena even forgot to miss Christy. Ray would be executing some complicated, verbal riff (on the differences between potato chip brands, say, or why you always felt sorry for the monster in old movies), and Feena would jump in. Surprised at how natural it seemed, she'd argue or answer back, things she'd never have dared a few weeks ago.

Raylene would stop, do a double take, and then, often as not, laugh out loud, that fuzzy, horsy bray of hers. "You are too much," she'd tell Feena. "Way too much." And there would be this look between them. This look that let each other in and kept everyone else out. Once in a while, though, the look would last too long, and they'd remember. They'd stop laughing, then, and they'd both remember Christy.

By Thursday, the once-in-a-whiles had started popping up all day long like weeds. When the final bell rang, Feena was glad to empty her locker and break for daylight. Beside her, Raylene dragged, her beautiful walk slow and heavy. "It's the same every day," she said. "My dumb feet don't know any better; they just want to head down to that old boat."

"I know."

"Only there's no point."

"No."

"Sometimes a week can seem like a year."

Feena nodded, then stopped. "Maybe there is a point," she said.

"What?" Raylene was feeling so sorry for herself, she didn't even glance up, just kept moving in that dispirited, halting way that made her look like a stranger, like someone else.

"Maybe we *could* go back to the boat." Feena followed after her now. "You know"—she paused, shy for the first time in weeks—"just the two of us?"

Now Raylene stopped, too. "What for?"

"To read." Feena felt foolish. "To talk and stuff." *How pathetic can I be? It's only Christy that keeps us together. Without him, why would Raylene want?...*

But Raylene was smiling. "You mean, hide out, anyway?"

Feena nodded.

"Let's get some soda first, okay?" The smile was a grin now.

So they changed direction, walked to the deli on the corner, then back across the soccer field to their secret trail through the woods. The afternoon was Florida at its best, a sort of lazy heat with breezes in the shade. At the sight of the clearing where the boat waited, Feena felt happier than she'd been in days.

"It's almost as if it was all meant to happen," she said, snug in the familiar galley, unpacking the soda and the Little Debbies they'd bought. She handed Ray one of the gooey cakes, a treat they would never have allowed Christy to eat. "Sugar rots your teeth," Raylene had declared, and that was that.

"What do you mean?" Raylene tore open the

wrapper on her cake. She, too, looked happier, more relaxed than she had all week. She sat in her old place on one side of the galley table, her long legs bridging the gap between them, her sandaled feet crossed on the bench by Feena.

"I mean, my mom getting this job in Florida. The Pizza Hut, Ryder's—everything."

"So?"

"So it was the only way we'd end up taking care of him, the two of us." Feena opened her own cake, took a bite, thought. "Like, when you look back at things you hated? Sometimes they make a sort of sense."

"And sometimes they don't." Raylene took a sip of her trademark orange soda, then sat frowning, thoughtful. "You know what I named my second sister?"

"What?"

"The one we'd already named, she was Dinah, after my grandmother. But I picked the other name all by myself." She grinned, remembering. "First, I thought about calling her Barbie, on account of the doll on that lamp." Raylene balled up her Little Debbie wrapper. "Or Patrice," she said, kneading the ball of paper between her palms. "I always liked that name.

"But then I remembered how long my mom and I had been waiting. How we'd scraped and painted and planned. So I just wrote Hope instead of all the fancy things I'd thought about. Hope. Isn't that some name for a dead baby?"

"I think it's beautiful. And I'm so sorry, Ray."

"It happened a long time ago."

"No." Feena smoothed the table, studied the whorls in the rough wood as if they were hieroglyphs. "I mean, I'm sorry about Christy." She looked up at Raylene now. "Here you took care of him and me. You cut school and ditched work. You broke the law right along with us, and never complained once."

"Look, that isn't—"

"And how did I repay you? I went and took Christy home without even telling you. I—"

"Will you be quiet?" Raylene threw her Little Debbie ball across the galley, missing the plastic bag they'd hung on a peg. "There's something I didn't tell you, too. Something I thought you figured out, on account of you're so smart."

"What?"

"Just that I don't do stuff unless I want to, that's all. I like hanging with you. See?"

Yes. Feena did see. In a shy rush of joy, a moment in which she hardly dared look at the other girl, Feena realized what she should have known all along. What she should have sensed under the jive and the teasing, the fast talk and the sweet walk. Raylene was her friend.

nineteen

.

.

.

By Friday, Feena's and Raylene's spirits had brightened considerably. Raylene even suggested they go shopping after school. "I figure we'll get Toffee some new books," she said. "I read that piano story so many times, I learned how to play!" She ran her supple fingers up and down the keyboard of an air piano.

"And let's buy some overalls, too," Feena rhapsodized. "Wouldn't he look adorable in them?"

"Uh-huh." Raylene nodded. "It's about time he found out he's a boy."

So they stopped by the Pizza Hut long enough for Feena to sweet-talk Lenore out of her credit card, then took the bus to what passed for a mall in Washanee—a department store, a shoe store, two outlets, and a Pasta Palace. It was almost like playing house, looking at the rows of baby outfits on little plastic hangers, debating colors, arguing over prices.

"I already spent last week's paycheck," Raylene scolded when Feena dragged her into Step Ahead. "I'm not about to blow this week's on cowboy boots the size of my thumb."

"But look how cute." Feena picked one of the tiny boots up, turned it so Raylene could see the cactus and the eagle stitched across the toe. "He loves blue."

They settled on sneakers instead. Blue, of course. They found shorts and overalls and three shirts—one Raylene liked, one Feena chose, and one that had a polar bear on the front. They bought books, and building blocks, and a set of sand toys, complete with a pail, shovel, and rake.

Feena was eyeing a bright yellow backhoe and a dollhouse family when Raylene called a halt. "Number one," she said, "who's going to carry all this stuff; and number two, who's going to play with it?"

When Feena continued to cradle the dollhouse mother, smoothing its skirt and hair, Raylene took it gently out of her hands. "Come on," she said. "Let's go home and play with our toys."

"Okay." Feena brightened, then followed her friend out of the store. "Mom will get a kick out of seeing all this stuff."

"I didn't mean *that* home," Raylene told her.

"Huh?"

"You know how we always told your mama you were spending the night at my house?"

Feena nodded, filling with hope.

"Well, how about you do it for real this time?" Raylene sounded almost shy. "If you want to, I mean."

Feena liked Raylene's mother, liked her throaty laugh, and the way she exclaimed over the things they'd bought. Liked the way she put a candle by each of their beds that night. Raylene's was green, and Feena's was gold. They made a little ceremony out of lighting them, then talked until both of them were dizzy with exhaustion.

Most of all, though, Feena liked the cheese grits Mrs. Watson cooked Saturday morning. The lush smell of it, the eddy-fingers of butter coasting across the thick ooze, were exotic, new to her. When she remembered, Lenore left bagels or English muffins in the refrigerator for breakfast. And she usually had Feena put them in the toaster, since half the time she'd end up burning them when she did it herself. "If you wanted Mother Goose," she used to say defensively, "you grew up in the wrong house."

After breakfast, Feena and Raylene spent the rest of the morning asking each other what time it was. Until ten o'clock. "Anybody with kids," Raylene said at last, "has *got* to be up by now." They decided, finally, to bring only half of what they'd bought with them this first trip. They didn't want to spoil Christy, and they could always bring more presents next week.

They rushed all the way to Bide A Bit, then slowed down, like shy suitors, once they'd reached the entrance sign by the palms. They were juggling packages and arguing over who would give what to Christopher when Feena stopped a few yards short of the blue trailer. Stopped and stared. Something was wrong.

The plastic geranium and pot were missing from the stoop, but that wasn't what made her heart lurch when she looked at the doublewide. It was the windows. There were no blinds in them, and where she'd had to peek through slats, she could now look right into the empty living room. No furniture. No piano. No pictures on the wall.

Raylene let her bags fall, ran up close to the front window. Feena watched her friend's head drop, her fists clench. The moan she heard then was a little like Raylene's songs, only harsher, deeper, like someone trying to catch her breath.

Feena wondered if this was like drowning. As she stood there, listening to Raylene moan and watching the morning sun glint off the vacant windows, a hundred pictures shuffled through her brain. They were like snapshots, like the photos she'd looked at with her mother. But these pictures were not of her brother; they were of the other Christy, the little boy she'd taken back to this trailer just last week.

Every minute, every day she'd spent with him came back to her now. Came back in frozen memories, tiny colored scenes ready to paste in a scrapbook: Christy digging in the sandbox; Christy checking his bunny dress for blue; Christy grabbing her hand, begging for "mik"; Christy triumphantly resurrecting his favorite book from a pile; Christy, his face darkened, his arms raised to protect his head; Christy, eyes closing as a story put him to sleep.

At first, Feena didn't know who was crying. Raylene turned around, her stricken face a question mark, and Feena thought maybe it was Raylene who was sobbing so loudly. But then, when the older girl walked toward her, when Feena felt her own body shaking like a bad dance in Raylene's arms, she knew it must be her. "They took him," she heard herself say. "They took him away."

But Raylene, her jaw set, was already steering them next door. She rang the doorbell of the small white trailer that shared a driveway with the doublewide. "Excuse me," she said when a slim girl with a wispy ponytail answered the door. "Can you tell me what happened to the family next door?"

"Not for sure," the girl told her. "Maybe Mom knows." She turned around and screamed into the back of the house. "Mom! Someone to see you." An older, thinner woman materialized behind the girl, and Raylene repeated her question.

"I know the same as everyone else," the woman told Raylene. "They were noisy and dirty and no good. I'm not exactly crying, now they're gone."

"You know where they went?"

"Nope."

Feena, who hadn't spoken, who had stood stunned and useless beside her friend, remembered something Delores had said. She forced herself to ask about it now. "She mentioned this cousin in Atlanta." Her hopes were rising like a foolish sun. It was either that or start crying again. "Do you think they went there?"

"Maybe. They didn't leave no forwarding address." The woman half smiled. "Just a mess of beer cans."

"Did they all go together?" Delores had said she'd leave if she got a job. Feena called back the sweaty determined face, the dreamy young voice. "Did Christy's father go with them?"

The woman's smile was more like a grimace, the face you make when a Band-Aid's pulled off. "That wasn't his father, honey. And I doubt that lug could travel past the nearest bar." The woman looked hard at the two girls over her daughter's shoulder. "What you want to know all this for, anyway? You social workers or something?"

"No," Raylene told her.

"Was he crying?" Feena asked.

"Who?"

"Christy," Feena said. "Christy, her little boy."

"I couldn't say, honey." The woman stared past them out the door. "Listen here, Lisa Ann. Didn't you say you finished sweeping that walk? Looks to me, you finished before you started."

The thin girl moved away from the door. "Mo-om," she said, stretching the word into two syllables. "Give it a rest."

The woman shrugged, continued. "That little kid? He coulda been laughing or crying, all I know. They left in the middle of the night." She paused. This time there was no smile. "That kind always do."

When they had knocked on all the other neighbors' doors and learned nothing new, nothing to pin the slimmest of hopes on, Feena and Raylene left Bide A Bit. They walked, wordlessly, as if they'd arranged it ahead of time, toward the old boat. They reached it just as the sun had found the stern and was poking long streamers of light through the cabin's louvered doors. They sat inside, facing each other across the table, the bags of new clothes and toys between them.

Neither girl spoke, and the only sound was the water, nibbling at the sides of the boat. Raylene pulled a shirt out of one bag, ran her finger along the grinning elephant on its front. "They found that other baby," she said at last.

Feena looked up, pretending an interest she didn't, couldn't feel.

"It was in the paper. Mama showed it to me while you were getting dressed." Raylene stopped her finger iron for a minute, smiled bitterly. "I got so excited about seeing Toffee, I forgot to tell you."

Feena said nothing.

"Turns out, it wasn't kidnapping at all, or not exactly. Turns out, the kid's dad took him. Anyway, he's home again."

"Good," Feena said, on automatic. "That's good." She turned her attention to the other bag, pulled out some books, the shovel and pail. "I never should have taken him back," she said now, staring at the toys in front of her, not at Raylene. "I should have gone to the police. That would have been the right thing."

"Right? This mess has gone way past right and wrong." Raylene sounded tired, numb. "The police and the fixer-uppers don't have all the answers, either. They make mistakes, too."

"But what if she's still hurting him?" Feena studied the pail she'd chosen, the octopus hugging a starfish.

She squinted, focusing on that cartoon hug. "What if she doesn't stop smoking? What if she—"

"What-ifs work both ways." Raylene had started ironing again, her hands passing back and forth, back and forth, over the tiny shirt. "What if it's the beginning instead of the end? What if it's the best for everyone, starting over like this?" She brushed under one eye, forced herself to look hopeful. "What if Toffee's mom has gone and done what you said? What if she's found that second chance? Grabbed it and kept on running?"

Feena sat still, head bent. "I can't stop thinking about him, Ray. I can't stop picturing him in my mind." She lifted her eyes to Raylene's now but held tight to the pail as if it might jump out of her hands. "You know how patient Christy is? How he'll sit where you tell him? Well, I keep seeing him, his hair in his eyes, his mouth moving like water the way it does. I see him just sitting there, waiting for you and me to come back and get him."

"I hope he thinks about us some." Raylene's voice was husky, lower than usual, and Feena saw the shine in her eyes. "But I hope he doesn't wait."

"No." Raylene was right; Feena knew that. You couldn't spend your life looking behind you, waiting for someone who'll never come back. "Do you think he's too young to remember?"

"I remember a song my grandmother used to sing."

"So?"

"So I wasn't much older than Toffee when she died." Raylene waved a mosquito away, forgoing the usual execution-style swat. "I don't know a single word. But I can still hear the music, and I can still feel the feeling. I figure that's the kind of remembering Toffee might do."

"Is that enough?"

"I don't know. But sometimes a little is better than nothing at all. I mean, maybe there's no such thing as a fresh start. Maybe you can't live without hurting some. I keep thinking about that book you 'borrowed' from me."

Feena couldn't laugh. She couldn't even smile.

"Remember what Janie says when she and her man get caught in that flood? When he asks if she's sorry she ever met him?"

Feena thought back to the scene where the two lovers are huddled inside a tiny sharecropper's shack while a hurricane screams outside. How differently Jane's and Janie's stories had ended, one finding her lost love, the other living on memories. Was it asking too much for Christy's story to have a happy ending?

"She says she'd rather wake up to the sun, even if it's only for one day, than be fumblng around in the dark her whole life." Raylene slipped the shirt back in the bag. "I had more time with Christy than I did with my sisters. I'm not sorry."

"But what about Christy?" As waves mumbled underneath the deck and the sun shifted its bright attentions from the door to the window, Feena tried to see into the future. Numb with the loss of the little boy she'd known for weeks and loved for years, she wondered where Christy would grow up, who he would become.

"A few days, Ray. That's all we gave him."

"Days of peace. Space to breathe."

"But it wasn't real." Feena remembered the duck and the decoy, shook her head. "It was make-believe, way too short to last a lifetime."

"We did the best we knew. My guess is, it was the best he ever had."

Maybe it was, Feena thought. Maybe love, real or unreal, short or long, was better than none. And maybe Christy would remember those precious days, those few spins of the planet when she'd held him in her arms. But more, so much more it ached, she wanted the rest of his life to be easier than its start.

Another part of Raylene's book came back to her, the part where Janie talks to the tiny seeds as they're carried off on the wind. She whispered the words to herself now, like a charm or a prayer. "I hope," she told Christopher as the future plucked him up and whirled him away from her, "I hope you land on soft ground."

ACKNOWLEDGMENTS

A book isn't a book without readers. And those who take the time to read a book before it's published are among the most precious resources a writer has. This time around, I am especially grateful to Marc and Robin Jacobson, Amy Ehrlich, Karen Lotz, Norma Fox Mazer, Marion Dane Bauer, Jim Van Cleve, and last but not least, my five cohorts in crime, the Picayune Writers. Thank you, one and all.

I wrote *Waiting for Christopher* to tell a story, Feena's story. A character popped into my head, and I was off and running—that's how all my books begin.

In order to write Feena's book, though, I had to do research on abused children, real children who need their stories told, too. I learned that abuse is a vicious cycle and that most abusive parents were once abused children. The key, of course, is to prevent abuse before it happens, to teach new mothers and fathers to be effective, loving parents.

But sometimes it's too late for prevention. Sometimes a child's safety or life is at stake. What should you do if you see a child in danger? First, I hope you'll educate yourself about child abuse. The website of Prevent Child Abuse America (www.preventchildabuse.org) is a good place to start. Second, to get help in your area, use the national hotline established by Childhelp USA: 1-800-4A-CHILD.

Louise Hawes has written fourteen novels for middle graders and young adults. While living in the northeast, she received two New Jersey Writing Fellowships and the New Jersey Author's Award. She is a founding faculty member of the nation's first MFA in Writing for Children program at Vermont College. Her short fiction has appeared in anthologies and journals in the United States and Canada.

Relocated to North Carolina, Louise Hawes currently lives in the Chapel Hill area. Her novel *Rosey in the Present Tense* has been nominated for the South Carolina YA Book Award 2001–2002.

For more information about the author, visit her website at http://www.louisehawes.com.